THEO

SILVER TEAM
BOOK 1

RILEY EDWARDS

BE A REBEL
Riley Edwards Romance

THEO
Silver Team 1

Cover design: Lori Jackson Designs

Written by: Riley Edwards

Published by: Riley Edwards/Rebels Romance

Edited by: Rebecca Hodgkins

Proofreader: Julie Deaton

Book Name: THEO

Paperback ISBN: 9798854183208

First edition: July 27, 2023

for Becca

fly high Queen

You will be forever missed.

xoxo

CONTENTS

1

I WAS LIVING A NIGHTMARE OF MY OWN MAKING.

My life had been erased, my past rewritten, my name changed, my medical records, credit and job history, education—all wiped clean. I had nothing from my previous life. Not a picture of my parents, not a movie stub, not a birthday card from my sweet Grandma Margie. Nothing. All gone. Sometimes I wondered about what had been done with all my stuff. Was it taken to a landfill and thrown in the trash? Was it taken somewhere and burned? And the most disturbing part was how easy it had been for someone sitting behind a computer to delete my whole life.

I was no longer Bridget Keller.

Though I wasn't thinking any of those thoughts now as I fought for my life. As pathetic as it had become, I still didn't want to die. Especially not like this.

I felt the man straddling my hips tighten his grip around my neck. My struggling did very little to stop the pads of his fingers from digging into my flesh, robbing me of much-needed oxygen.

"Last chance, Bridget. What did you see?"

Just like the three other times the man had asked before he tackled me to the floor, I had no answer, and if I did I wouldn't have been able to give it, seeing as he was strangling me. Which was scarier than when he'd slapped me—and at the time that had been pretty damn scary... and painful. I'd never been hit by a man or, well, anyone, and let's just say the sting of the slap hurt worse than I'd imagined. Mercifully by the third time he'd landed his palm on my face my cheek had gone numb. Or maybe at some point, pain was pain and adding more didn't matter when the agony was already such that it stole your breath.

"Answer. Me!" he screamed in my face.

I would've flinched or jerked my head away as spittle landed on my forehead if he didn't have one hand wrapped around my throat and the other fisting my hair, yanking it so hard I thought he was going to pull it out by the roots.

The corners of my vision darkened.

I was running out of time.

The man was too big and heavy. All the bucking and kicking and twisting was in vain.

I'd given up everything to do the right thing and this was how I was going to die.

Months of living in safe houses, months of no privacy, months of being questioned by prosecutors prepping for trial, months of misery that I knew would lead to giving up a normal future and this was how it was going to end.

A man I'd never seen before on top of me strangling me to death.

Alone.

In a house that had been given to me by the government as payment for my good deed.

All for nothing.

I should've kept my mouth shut. I would've hated myself but at least I would've been alive.

"What's going on in here?"

I knew that voice.

The man on top of me shifted his weight. He tipped his head back to look at my neighbor who was approximately a hundred and five, and now was my chance. I quickly bent my knees, put the soles of my bare feet on the carpet, and with all the strength I could muster, thrust my hips up and twisted, freeing my pinned hands.

"Get off her!" Flix shouted.

The hand around my neck loosened. Oxygen filled my lungs, which in turn gave me a fighting chance. A chance I wasn't going to squander—so fight I did. I clawed at his face, arched, reared, and shoved. In other words I launched an attack, putting the man on top of me off balance until I forced him off of me.

I scrambled to my feet at the same time as my assailant, drawing in one painful lungful of air after another and preparing for another battle. Thankfully that battle never came. The man turned tail and ran through the living room into the kitchen and out the back door.

"Are you okay, Brenda?" Flix asked.

Flix.

Thank God for my elderly neighbor.

I whirled around and took in his wrinkled face. Normally it was full of kindness and humor but right then he looked pale and fearful. I didn't know the man well. I hadn't lived next to him long enough to form a bond, however, I had sat in his kitchen and listened to him share stories about his deceased wife and children. I knew he had grandchildren. I knew he was losing his eyesight but, and I quote, "the good Lord has sharpened my hearing" and thank God He did.

Incidentally I had shared nothing with Flix. Not that I had anything to share—after all, I'd only been Brenda King a few months and Brenda had no life experience beyond the cover WITSEC gave her. And for some reason it didn't seem right to share those made-up stories with a man who had offered me kindness and generosity.

"I'm..." I stopped to clear my scratchy throat. "I'm fine."

"I called the police."

Oh, shit.

I couldn't be here when the police arrived.

I couldn't be here at all.

They found me.

Whoever *they* were.

Without hesitation I ran to the side table I always set my purse on and snatched it on my way to the front door, only stopping long enough to pull Flix's frail body into a brief hug.

"Thank you, Flix, I'll never forget you. You saved my life."

I let go and was running out the door when I heard him yelling after me. Guilt immediately clawed at my insides—not that I could do anything about it. Just like all the regret that weighed heavily, the guilt, too, would have to sit in my belly until I learned to live with it.

Barefoot in my car, or rather the car I'd been given—

one over which I had no choice in color, make, or model, therefore it was a boring white sedan that I was told was non-conspicuous and safe—I peeled out of the driveway of a house that I would never see again. I left behind all of the shit I'd been given that I hadn't wanted in the first place and headed to the one person I knew could help me.

Theo.

A mile down the road I threw my government-issued cell phone out the window. I wasn't stupid, I knew everything I had was being tracked. At this point I wouldn't have been surprised to find out that I'd been drugged and a subcutaneous GPS device had been implanted. And since I wasn't stupid, I'd spent a lot of time driving around getting the lay of the land. Clarksville, New York, was beautiful. I wouldn't have picked it as a place to live and it certainly wasn't what I was used to but it was quaint and it did have cute mom-and-pop shops and a kickass diner with the best milkshakes I'd ever had, and the people who lived in Clarksville were friendly. But I couldn't say I'd miss it, except for Flix. I'd miss him.

I turned onto Tarrytown Road and did my best to take in the beautiful fields, the corn just peeking up out of the dirt, the trees, the cute farmhouses, knowing I'd never see any of this again. Eventually Tarrytown Road ended and I took a right onto 32, the highway that would lead me to freedom. Or at least to a truck stop and if luck was on my side, I'd hitch a ride with a nice, non-creepy trucker who would take me to Maryland.

A few hours later, I learned luck wasn't on my side as I rode next to a man who was nice, non-creepy, but talkative in a way that made me wish I had the option to go to sleep or at least pretend I was. But I wasn't dumb and I knew I'd already taken a huge risk—necessary, since I figured my car had a tracking device on it, but still an enormous risk—getting into a truck with a stranger. I wasn't going to take any further chances. So there I was listening to Troy the Trucker tell me about the time he'd been abducted by aliens. Not that he'd called them aliens, he referred to his captures as "celestial beings".

"...but it wasn't all bad," he finished. "I'd go back if I was invited."

I didn't take my eyes off the road when I said, "Well, that's good."

"So tell me about yourself, Cindy."

Cindy, that was me, or the new me I'd made up on the fly when Troy had asked my name.

Coming up with a fake name was harder than one would think. I should've prepared for the question but at the time I was just happy a semi had pulled into the deserted Fuel Hub gas station ten minutes after I'd gotten there. Which had given me just enough time to get my backpack out of the trunk, put on a pair of shoes, and hunt for all the cash I'd hidden in the car.

I'd heard people say, life was a crazy ride and nothing was guaranteed, or was that Eminem who said that? Anyway, it was the truth. A year ago I was coasting through life, not wildly happy but content. Now I was rummaging through a car to find wads of cash I'd stashed just in case—the just in case being running for my life with all of my worldly possessions shoved into a backpack. So, yes, life was a crazy ride I wanted desperately to jump off of.

I did not want this as my life.

Yet here I was in a truck with Troy after hitchhiking.

Awesome.

"Nothing to tell," I lied.

Troy's chuckle was an obvious indication he knew I wasn't telling the truth so really it was unnecessary for him to comment, but Talkative Troy had a comeback, "You're not the first woman I've picked up who was on the run and I hate to tell you this, Cindy, but you all look the same."

Well, damn.

An unwelcomed shame washed over me.

"I'm not in trouble with the law or anything."

"Wouldn't care if you were," he told me.

That got my attention, as well as my gaze, and I really needed to keep my eyes on the road but I couldn't stop myself. What kind of man didn't care if he was aiding and abetting a criminal? Other than his stories about being abducted by friendly aliens he seemed normal. He certainly looked normal but maybe Trucker Troy was really Outlaw Troy and that was worrisome.

"You wouldn't care?"

"Nope. Not my place to judge. Sometimes good people are forced to do bad things. Or things that are considered wrong but they had no choice. Sometimes people are just dicks and do bad things because that's what dicks do and I wouldn't have let you in my truck if I thought you were a dick. So if you're running from the law, well, you had a good reason for doing whatever it is you did."

"I could be a dick," I mumbled.

"I can sniff a dick from a hundred miles away."

I couldn't stop my junior high self from making an appearance and snickering at his comment.

"You can sniff...a...dick," I stammered around a giggle.

"And that right there, is why I know you're not running from the law."

Troy reached over and patted my shoulder. It was not creepy or weird, or anything but something a nice person would do.

I relaxed a little in my seat and told him a little bit of the truth. "I just need to get to Annapolis and then I'll be safe."

"Then Annapolis is where we're going," he returned.

"You said you could get me to Philly. That's far enough—"

"I'm taking you to Annapolis."

I wanted to argue but I didn't. I needed help and if Troy wanted to go out of his way to get me to Theo I wasn't going to turn him down.

"Thank you."

"I'd tell you to close your eyes and take a nap but you don't strike me as stupid so I know you won't."

He was correct. I wasn't stupid and there was no way I was closing my eyes.

"I hope that doesn't offend you."

"It doesn't but we're stopping to get you some ice for your swollen cheek. Now, if you bitch about the detour, *that* I will find offensive."

At the mention of my cheek my hand went to my face.

"And tell me something, Cindy, the person who put those marks on your neck..." Troy let that hang.

Shit. I hadn't looked at myself in the mirror. I had no idea there were marks on my neck though it made sense seeing as I was almost choked to death.

"The reason I wasn't safe," I answered.

Talkative Troy turned into Silent Troy as he drove to the next gas station. It wasn't until he parked his rig that he turned in my direction and scowled.

"I debated asking you this again since you misunderstood the first time but I have to know. The person who did that to you, did he get his?"

For the first time since I got into the truck I was freaked out, really and truly freaked out. Not weirded out by stories of celestial beings, not worried my kidnapping and subsequent death-by-truck driver would be inspiration for the next *CSI* episode, but freaked out because Troy looked irate.

Not at me. At the person who hurt me.

I also understood his question this time.

So I answered, "No. He got away."

"Shame. A piece of shit who puts his hands on a woman at a minimum deserves a beat down."

And with that he got out of the truck.

I watched as he walked toward the gas station store. I did this thinking I was wrong earlier. Luck had been on my side when I found Troy.

"I DON'T LIKE THIS," Troy said as he looked around the no-name motor inn.

I didn't like it either but I had limited funds and still had to buy a junker car to get me around until I could find Theo.

I wasn't sure how I was going to do that since I was

pretty sure my new identity could be tracked, and using my old name wasn't an option beyond the obvious reason that when you entered witness protection they took all your old documents and did whatever they did with all your belongings.

Maybe getting taxis to take me around would be a better option.

"Can you pay for taxis with cash?"

Troy emitted a grumble that sounded an awful lot like a growl before he answered begrudgingly, "Yes."

Okay, that was good.

Tomorrow I would have a taxi take me to... where? One of the safe houses I stayed at? I was pretty sure those weren't recycled, waiting for the next federal witness to use.

"I didn't think this through," I mumbled.

"Think what through?"

Without thinking I told the truth, "How to find him."

"Him?"

I was exhausted, traumatized, and the day had finally hit me.

From the moment the attack started I'd gone into survival mode. Then when I was free, autopilot kicked in and I did everything I'd taught myself to do.

I got myself safe.

But now six hours later sitting in Troy's truck outside of the motel everything came crashing down around me. The fear, the anxiety, the dread, the panic, the terror that I'd been able to shove to the side was no longer possible. I couldn't remember what it was like not to be afraid.

"The man I need to find to get me safe," I told him

through tears. "He's here, in Annapolis. I just don't know how to find him."

"You're killing me, sweetheart. It's not my place to hug you, but damn if I don't want to."

He was right, it wasn't his place; he was a stranger. Or he had been six hours ago when he'd picked me up. Now he felt like a long-lost uncle. Not that I knew what having an uncle was like. My mom only had sisters and none of them were very nice. And I'd never met my father or any of his family. But Troy was what I imagined a good uncle would be like.

I prided myself on being smart—not book smart but street smart. But I couldn't stop myself from doing something stupid. After everything that had happened today I needed something...kindness, connection, a little bit of compassion, even if it was from someone who I didn't know. I unclasped my hands resting in my lap and reached across the cab of the truck and covered Troy's hand resting on the gear shifter. As soon as I did, his other hand landed on top of mine and he patted it.

That was it. That was all I needed. Just a kind gesture from a man who had gone out of his way to help me.

"My name's not Cindy." I continued to be stupid. "But I can't tell you my real name."

I didn't know why I blurted that out other than it felt wrong lying to Troy.

He ignored my confession to ask, "How firm are you about staying in this place?"

I stopped staring at our hands and looked up to find concern etched in his weathered face.

"Firm."

"Right. Would it freak you out if I got the room next to you?"

Yes. But not for the reasons it should. I found nothing creepy about his offer. But his kindness freaked me plenty.

"You don't—"

"I know I don't but I want to. If that's going to make you uncomfortable I'll stay in my sleeper." Troy jerked his head to the side, indicating the sleeping area behind us.

"Really, you've done enough," I protested. "You have someplace to be."

There was a long stretch of silence before Troy finally broke it.

"I have a daughter. I'd like to think if she was in a tight spot someone out there would help her. I also have a son. He's real good with computers. He works for some of those fancy internet companies. Maybe he can help you find who you're looking for."

I didn't miss the softness in his tone when he mentioned his daughter or the pride when he spoke of his son. His offer was a godsend but I couldn't accept it.

As if sensing I was going to deny his help he made a suggestion. "I'll give you my driver's license. You can take a picture with your phone and send it to a friend. I think that's what women do nowadays to keep themselves safe on those dating apps."

I would've smiled at his obvious disdain for those 'dating apps' if I wasn't in the middle of a poorly thought-out plan. How the hell I messed up the last and biggest piece of the puzzle I'd never know. It hadn't occurred to me that I didn't know where to find Theo.

And since I'd already been stupid I continued down that path when I admitted, "I don't have a phone."

That sounded better than admitting I didn't have a single friend I could send his information to.

"You don't have a phone?" he asked incredulously. "Do you know how incredibly unsafe that is?"

Yes, I knew, but being tracked by my phone was more unsafe than not having one.

I nodded my response. Troy narrowed his eyes and sighed.

That made me want to smile again. He was giving off pissed-off-dad vibes instead of the kind uncle vibes he'd been giving me the last few hours.

"That does it. We're calling Lewis. I'll step out of the truck. You tell him who you're looking for and he'll help you."

He said that like it was a done deal and he didn't need to ask his son if he wanted to help. He also said it like...

Wait...

Lewis.

Zane Lewis.

That was Theo's boss. The only man who'd given me his last name when I was dropped off at the first safe house. He came in after the Marshals had left to introduce himself and explain that he and his team would be keeping me safe until the trial. I'd only seen him a few times. But Zane was not a man you forgot. Well, you didn't forget what his presence felt like; obviously his last name had escaped me.

"I know how to find him," I announced. "May I use your phone?"

"One condition," he demanded. "You don't pitch a fit

that I'm staying until I know you're safe. And by safe I mean I see with my own eyes you've found whoever you're looking for."

I took in Troy, really took him in. From his gray hair to his equally gray beard to his kind eyes. Then I remembered him stopping to get me ice for my face and snacks for the trip. After that I remembered he thought that any man who hit a woman deserved a minimum of a beat down. He'd seen my swollen cheek and the marks around my neck and he'd still offered me a ride even though there was a possibility I'd bring him trouble. No, he offered me a ride *because* he saw the marks on my face and he knew I was in trouble.

Plus, he could smell a dick a mile away.

"Deal."

Troy handed me his phone.

"I'm going in to book us rooms."

With that he jumped out of his truck, trusting me with his phone.

2

"IT'S GOOD TO SEE HER SMILING AND HAPPY," EASTON Spears, one of my teammates, said from beside me.

The "her" was Kira Winters, now Kira Cain, and Easton was wrong—it wasn't *good*, it was fucking fantastic. After everything that woman had been through, seeing her happy gave me hope. Kira was the poster child for shit luck. If it could go wrong it had.

She'd lost her entire family but had found the strength to not only overcome that grief but use it to fuel her ambition. She could've wallowed in her pain and no one would've blamed her, but instead she used it to flourish.

The woman was wicked smart, funny, and loyal. Cooper was a lucky son of a bitch but before he came along Kira Winters was ours—mine, Easton's, Smith's, Jonas's, Cash's, and Layla's. She was more than a teammate, more than the intel specialist, hacker, software designer. She was way more than my handler when I was out in the field. I loved that woman like a sister. So after knowing her more than ten years, knowing she was a lonely workaholic on a mission to prove herself, seeing her smiling and happy was everything.

But I didn't say any of that. It was unnecessary seeing as I knew Easton felt the same.

So instead I kept my eyes on the newly married couple swaying to some love song I didn't know in the middle of the dance floor and gave a simple, "Yep."

"What are you two doing?" Layla asked as she and Kevin stopped next to the bar where we were standing.

"I think he's," Easton shoved his thumb in my direction, "trying to blend into the wall so no one asks him to dance."

That was exactly what I was doing, minus the wall since my ass was out in the open at the bar, though I planned on correcting that oversight as soon as Easton got his drink and left.

"Me?" he continued, "I'm just waiting for my beer and the music to change so me and Cash can show you fuckers how to dance."

Easton and Cash would show the crowd something but it wouldn't be how to dance. It would be how to make an ass out of yourself.

I heard Kevin chuckle and glanced over at the man who had managed to claim my team leader, Layla. Much like Kira, Layla's intelligence was blade sharp. She could and had outsmarted war-harden terrorists. She was CIA-trained but the skills she had were not from her time at the CIA; she came by them naturally. Kevin was not lucky like Cooper, whereas despite what Kira had been through there was still a softness to her. Layla had protected herself by encasing her heart with barbed wire. Kevin had worked hard to uncover what was underneath all those razors before striking gold.

"You don't know how to dance," Layla reminded him.

"Says who?"

"Says the same people who tell you, you can't sing."

Easton snagged his fresh beer off the bar before raising it up in a salute.

"Do I look like a man who gives a shit what other people think?"

"Nope," I answered before Layla could.

"Correct." He smiled before bringing his beer to his mouth and guzzling half of it in one go.

Layla's laughter that followed was still startling. For the first ten years I knew the woman I'd never heard her laugh. That also counted the time I knew her before I'd faked my death and went undercover, before she'd taken on the task of sending five men out on dangerous missions attempting to uncover corruption that went so deep, that with each mission we'd learned we hadn't begun to scratch the surface.

The network we'd built all came crashing down when I'd been captured. Layla had pulled the plug and ten years went down the drain—all to save me.

The guilt of that still coursed through my veins like lava.

Not only did we lose everything, but Kevin and Zane had almost died trying to rescue me.

"It's a damn good thing Layla tossed out her rule book." Easton bumped my shoulder as he strode past, beer in hand, destination the dance floor. "Time to have some fun."

"Rule number seven," Kevin started. "No fun."

"No fun on *an op*," Layla corrected.

I couldn't say we'd had fun during our ops, but the guys and I had broken every rule Layla had put in place. She'd forbidden us to see each other between missions, though we regularly got together when we had downtime. None of us were allowed contact with anyone back in the States, yet Easton had reached out to Garrett Davis in an effort to mend fences. I couldn't think of a single rule we hadn't ignored. Working for Zane and Z Corps was proving to be much like working for Layla—there was a rule book in place, however, no one paid it any mind either, which gave my new boss and his Mini Me Kira fodder for ball breaking.

"Everything okay?"

At Layla's soft-spoken question my gaze went from watching Easton to her.

"Everything's great."

Her narrowed eyes told me exactly what she thought about my canned response.

"Theo—"

"Tonight we're celebrating Kira," I interrupted her. "Let's leave it at that, yeah?"

"As long as you know I'm worried about you."

Layla's veiled acquiescence hit me square in my chest. I didn't want her worried about me; she'd already spent ten years worried about me, Easton, Smith, Jonas, and Cash. She didn't need to waste any more time on us.

"It's all good, Layla."

"Have you talked to your brother?"

My brother, Bronson, was a sore subject. I didn't want

to discuss him today or any other day. But I knew I had to give her something.

"We're getting there."

By *there*, I meant he'd vowed to never speak to me again.

"I can talk to him," she offered. "Explain everything."

That was a hell no. My brother was rightfully pissed at me. He felt I betrayed him, and in a way I had. I'd hurt him, my stepfather, and my mother. Thankfully my parents understood why I'd done what I'd done. Bronson, on the other hand, did not.

"He needs time and I'm giving him that."

Thankfully Kevin handing Layla her drink ended the conversation.

"Are you joining us?" Kevin asked with a smirk, knowing damn good and well I wasn't going to sit with them at a table out in the open.

"Thanks but I'll pass."

"Afraid Kira will get you on the dance floor?"

"Yep."

"We'll leave you to it then," Kevin finished.

Layla reached over and squeezed my forearm before she followed Kevin back to their table. And there I was, right back to how I'd felt since I came home from ten years overseas—surrounded by people yet very much alone.

Alone with my thoughts.

Alone with my anger.

Alone with my misery.

Just. Alone.

An hour later, I was doing my best to hide in a corner so I didn't get pulled into the absurdity that was happening on the dance floor. What was supposed to be a choreographed line dance looked more like twenty people dancing to twenty different songs that the other people couldn't hear. For a group of men who could stealthily move together in perfect sync they couldn't dance for shit. Absolutely zero rhythm among the lot of them.

I felt a hand on my shoulder and mentally came up with a new excuse to give as to why I was not going to dance.

With a fake smile firmly in place I turned, ready with my explanation.

My excuse along with my smile died when I didn't find a happy partygoer as expected but instead a woman who should've been somewhere in middle-of-nowhere Nebraska, or Georgia, or California. Where she absolutely shouldn't have been was at Cooper and Kira's wedding reception in Maryland.

"What the hell are you doing here, Bridget?"

I watched as her eyes widened but my gaze went over her shoulder to the man standing behind her.

"I need your help." Her plea was barely audible over the thumping music.

Or was that my pounding heart I could feel roaring in my ears from seeing her again after I'd already mourned the loss of her, that made her request hard to hear?

Mourned might've been a slight overstatement but not by much. For months I'd guarded her. I'd spent hours and days with her and I'd denied myself what I'd wanted and kept every interaction professional. When she was taken from me and put into WITSEC I said nothing. I let her go knowing it was the only way she'd be safe but now there she was standing in front of me with a man who looked old enough to be her father behind her. Old and out of shape and no way was the man a Marshal or a bodyguard.

I blamed my next move on knowing her situation, on instinct, on the fact she should not have been anywhere near Maryland or me, so when I tagged her hand and yanked her to my side, shifted her behind me, and drew my weapon I felt no remorse when the man stepped back two feet.

Smart.

Bridget's hand went to my side, curled around, and her fingertips pressed into my ribs.

"Don't hurt him. He's a friend."

This man was no friend if he'd taken her from the safety of her new life.

"Explain that," I demanded.

"I will, but can we go somewhere private?"

Yeah, privacy would be good before one of my teammates saw her. Or worse, Zane.

"You." I used the barrel of my Sig to motion to the man. "Turn around and go out the door behind you. Turn left, go down the hall. Three doors down on the right there's an office."

The man frowned and ignored my instructions.

"You sure you can trust this guy?" the man asked.

"Yes," Bridget said from behind me.

Why did that feel so fucking good?

Of course she trusted me. I'd watched over her while she slept. I'd eaten dinner with her almost every night—lunch and breakfast, the same. I'd brought her groceries. I'd watched TV with her and sat quietly across the room while she'd read. I held her while she cried in frustration as the weeks had turned into months. Then, there was the trial, and I'd been there through that as well.

I'd been with her more than any of the other guys. She knew me—or at least she knew the man I'd shown her. Yet I knew everything about her, and not from some file I'd been given. Bridget Keller got talkative when she was bored. She'd been open and honest about her childhood—almost marrying her high school sweetheart, dropping out of college and why. I knew this woman better than any woman I'd ever dated.

Finally the man turned and did as I asked. Without thinking about it, I pulled Bridget to my side, put my arm around her shoulder, and tucked her close before I followed him down the hall.

We entered the small office and I still didn't let her go—and I wasn't going to think about why I wanted her at my side and how good it felt to have her there. I also wasn't going to think about how happy I was to see her again when it meant something had gone horribly wrong for her. Therefore I couldn't keep the anger out of my tone when I demanded again, "Explain why you're here."

"Would you mind putting that away?" the man asked.

"Not until I know who you are and why she's here," I returned.

"This is Troy," Bridget started. "He gave me a ride down here and helped me find you."

There was a lot to process from that one sentence yet it told me nothing. Bridget trembling at my side spoke to her fear but not who or what she was afraid of.

"That tells me nothing."

Silence ensued, which wasn't something I was used to when it came to her. The Bridget I knew was outspoken and had no issue speaking her mind. There had been many times in the months I'd been with her she'd expressed her dislike of moving from house to house. She'd argued and fought with me when I wouldn't allow her to do something she wanted, something that would unnecessarily put her in danger like swinging by the mall to shop on the way to a new safe house. She'd known my answer would be no, yet she'd still asked, because that was who she was. Bridget wasn't a go-with-the-flow type of woman. She wanted a say in her life, which made being under federal protection where she had none especially frustrating for her. But neither was the woman stupid—she'd understood why the safety procedures were put in place and she knew to follow them to a T which made her being back in Maryland all that more alarming.

Bridget wouldn't break protocol unless...

"Did someone find you?"

I felt her nod her answer against my chest.

Jesus fuck.

"Did someone hurt you?"

This time her answer was not in the form of a nod. Her entire body went stiff and she pressed deeper into my side.

"Who?"

Bridget's trembling turned into a full body quake.

"I don't know."

Troy's eyes narrowed on Bridget and I wasn't sure if that meant she was lying to me or if it was because she'd given him the same answer and depending on how much she told the man—which hopefully was nothing—her not knowing who hurt her would be confusing.

"I need to talk to her alone," I told Troy.

"Not a chance, bud. Not until I know she's safe with you and you'll take care of her."

I had to hand it to the man. I had height and muscle on him and you'd have to be blind not to see I could take him out, and doing so would have nothing to do with the Sig I was still holding.

"She's safe," I assured him.

"No offense, but I'm not so sure about that."

"Theo's right, Troy, I'm safe with him. He'll know what to do."

"Cindy—"

"I promise," Bridget cut him off.

Cindy?

Was that her new name? Fuck, I'd called her Bridget in front of this guy and he hadn't questioned the name change. Maybe she'd told him more than I'd hoped she had.

"I don't like this," he complained.

"I know you don't and I appreciate why," she softly told him. "I can never repay your kindness these last four days. You saved my life."

Four days?

What the fuck?

There was a stretch of silence, during which Troy's eyes were glued to Bridget. A frown grooved his face as he considered his next move. He obviously cared about Bridget so it was going to suck when I physically removed him from the office but I didn't have time for a lengthy debate about what was going to be happening next. I needed answers, then I needed to get Bridget to safety.

"I want you checking in," Troy requested.

"Okay."

"No," I corrected.

"Yes, Theo." She squeezed her arm around me. "I don't know when that will be, but either I'll check in or Theo will contact you."

"That's not going to happen."

As soon as the words left my mouth Bridget pushed away from me and crossed her arms over her chest.

There was the strong-willed woman I knew.

"He saved my life," she slowly enunciated.

Fuck. I was going to give in.

"Fine." I looked from Bridget to Troy who didn't look happy he was getting the boot. "I'll check in with you."

It took a moment for Troy to accept my answer but I knew he had when he looked around the desk, found a pen, and scribbled something onto a sticky note.

"Here." He handed me the hot pink square. "If you don't call me in forty-eight hours I'll be back."

I let the threat go but not the demand.

"I can't promise when I'll call until I understand what's going on."

Everything about Troy changed—his barrel chest expanded with an inhale, his frown turned into a pain-filled grimace, and his eyes went hard.

"I'll tell you what's going on," he snarled. "Four days ago I picked up a woman who had red marks around her throat and the makings of a swollen cheek and when I did, that woman became my responsibility. So no, I'm not leaving here without your promise you'll call me and not in a week. In two days. If I don't get that call I'm coming back with the police and something tells me you don't want that. But more, *Cindy* doesn't want that. If she did, she would've called them, not gone to a truck stop to hitchhike from New York to Maryland, putting herself in more danger by getting in a rig with a stranger. I don't know what's happening. I don't care what's happening beyond *she's* safe and *you're* gonna keep her that way."

With each word Troy spoke, my chest tightened.

Red marks around her neck.

The makings of a swollen cheek.

Hitchhiked.

Oh, yeah, my chest was burning and my lungs were on fire when I spat, "She's safe and she's gonna stay that way."

"Theo..." Bridget whispered.

My eyes skidded to her. Her arms were still crossed over her chest but she was now shrinking into herself.

Fuck no.

"You're safe, baby, yeah? You know I'll keep you safe."

Without hesitation she nodded.

I went back to studying the man who'd brought her to me and made a decision.

"I'll call you tomorrow." Then I tacked on, "I think you understand there's more going on here than a woman who was simply attacked. You calling the police will put her in more danger than you can imagine."

"I got that within the first hour I had her with me," he confirmed.

"Where's your stuff?" I asked Bridget.

"I only have this." She pulled the strap of the backpack she was wearing.

Christ.

I bit back the curse, opting to move the conversation forward.

"We'll walk you out," I told Troy and opened the door.

I waited until Troy passed me before I looked back at Bridget.

"Come here."

Bridget closed the space between us and stood in front of me with her eyes cast up. I wasn't sure which I saw more of: fear or relief. I chose to focus on the relief and what that said. It would take me a few days to wipe away the fear but that was priority number one. After that I'd contemplate the reasons why she ran to me and not her contact and the Marshal service.

But I'd already made up my mind about one thing—this time I wasn't letting her go without a fight.

3

WITH MY ARMS TIGHTLY WRAPPED AROUND TROY I whispered, "Thank you."

"You can thank me by staying safe and making sure he calls me."

I didn't know how it had happened but somehow in the four days I'd spent with Troy I'd come to care about him. He'd gone from a complete stranger to my savior. He'd made me feel comfortable and safe but most of all he'd kept his word and got me to Theo.

"Theo knows what to do," I assured him for what felt like the five-hundredth time, but in reality it was probably only the tenth time. "And he'll call you, I promise."

Troy squeezed me tighter and in a gruff, dad-voice he said, "I don't want to leave you, sweetheart, but I know I need to let you go. Stay smart, and *you* call me if you need anything. I'll come and get you."

I totally believed that. If I needed Troy and called him he'd drive across the country to get to me.

"I will."

We were both silent as our hug lingered a few more seconds before breaking apart. I held my breath and waited as Troy eyed Theo skeptically. I couldn't know for sure but from what I did know about Theo, he wasn't the kind of man who would take kindly to being threatened, and Troy had already done that once. I hoped he didn't piss Theo off by doing it again. I needed his help out of the current mess I was in and unlike last time, the feds wouldn't be footing the bill. I didn't know how much Z Corps charged for their service but I did know whatever the fee was I couldn't pay it. So I needed Theo to help me for free and Troy making him angry wasn't going to help my situation.

Thankfully their silent exchange remained silent and whatever Troy felt he needed to communicate was done with a look and dip of his chin. Theo must've understood if the tilting of his chin in response was anything to go by. We watched as Troy walked to his car and got in.

"I thought he picked you up at a truck stop," Theo rumbled.

"He did."

"He said you got in his *rig*."

I contemplated lying to Theo, seeing as his voice was already gruff and full of anger. But it would be no use when the truth would come out later.

"He did. Two days ago, we drove up to Pittsburgh to deliver his haul. After that we went to Hershey where he lives and dropped off his rig and picked up his car. Driving a semi around Annapolis isn't exactly easy."

"You went to that man's house?" he growled.

Yep, Theo was angry.

"I can see why you'd think that wasn't smart," I easily

conceded. "But I trust him. And when I tell you the story you'll understand why."

I could barely make out Theo's features in the dim lighting of the parking lot but I didn't miss the way his dark eyes flashed. I'd seen that squinty look before. Actually, I'd seen it every time I'd challenged him, which was to say a lot. In the months he'd been my bodyguard I'd pushed the limits of the rules he'd put in place. Or maybe they weren't his rules; he was just the one who'd been in charge of enforcing them and I didn't like not having a say beyond what I was going to eat for the day. Thinking back I'd probably been bitchy at times and that was why Theo had been so closed off.

Coming to Maryland and asking him for help had been presumptuous.

"I'm sorry, Theo."

Theo's head tipped to the side.

"Why are you sorry?"

For everything.

Absolutely everything.

I wished I could go back and decline the job that had started this whole mess. Then I wouldn't have been put in a situation where I'd had to decide to do the right thing, but in doing so given up my future.

"I wasn't very nice to you—"

"Your whole life had been taken from you."

He wasn't wrong about that.

"And that makes it okay?"

"No, what it makes it, is understandable. But how about we shelve that conversation and get you someplace safe so you can tell me what's going on."

That sounded like a good idea. Actually it sounded brilliant because in all of my what-if preparation, and planning escape routes, and stashing money in my car in case of an emergency, I never once stopped to think about how I'd feel when I came face-to-face with Theo. I couldn't say I'd fallen in love with him, but I'd certainly been attracted to him. And there had been a couple of times when I'd mistaken his frustration with me as sexual tension, but that was only after I'd been separated from him for a few weeks and had reflected on our time together.

"Should we go back to the office?"

"No. We're going to a hotel for the night."

"A hotel?"

"Yes."

Um...

"Is that safe? Shouldn't we—"

"There is no safer place for you to be than with me."

The vehemence in his tone made me a believer, more so than I already was. There was a reason I'd run to Theo. I knew he'd help me; I knew he was a good, decent man, but the intensity behind his words was something else, something more and it rendered me speechless.

"Cindy, you'll be safe with me," he unnecessarily reiterated.

"I hate this," I grumbled.

"What part do you hate?"

All of it.

But right then, I hated the crazy, confusing name changes.

"You calling me Cindy."

"I get that," he returned in a way that told me he actually understood, then he swept his hand to the left. "Come on, let's go."

I sucked in a fortifying breath and followed Theo across the parking lot to a sleek, metallic gray BMW. When he opened the door for me I glanced from the car to Theo then back to the car. Unfortunately he didn't miss this which prompted him to ask, "What's wrong?"

The question was unfortunate because my answer gave away more than I wanted.

"I always imagined you driving a pickup or maybe an SUV."

A slow teasing smile I'd never seen coming from Theo played on his lips before it became smug.

"So you admit you thought about me."

I felt my face heat in the cool night breeze.

"I never said I didn't."

What in the world was I doing flirting with Theo?

Was that even flirting?

"Slide in, baby."

Now was he flirting back with me?

And *baby*? That was the second time he'd called me that. (Yes, I was counting.)

With nothing left to say I swung my backpack off. Theo took it from me and I slid in. Once inside, the new car smell assaulted me. I folded my hands, placed them on my lap, and I sat perfectly still. I knew nothing about cars but the supple black leather under my ass screamed expensive. Not to mention the chrome accents. Hell, even the rearview mirror was super fancy.

I was no less settled when Theo opened his door, tossed my backpack into the back seat of his luxury ride like it was a 1977 Pinto, and got in. As soon as he slammed his door closed he turned to look at me.

"What's wrong?" he immediately asked.

"Wrong?"

"Yeah, what's wrong? You're sitting there with your hands in your lap and your back straight. Do you need to adjust the seat?"

Was he nuts?

"Um, you have a nice car."

Theo blinked before he slowly said, "Okay."

"I don't want to mess it up."

Another blink, this time faster.

"Are you planning on eating a Big Mac in here and spilling it all over the seats?"

"Of course not."

"Dumping a Slurpee on the floor?"

I hadn't had a Slurpee in years.

"Are you planning on swinging by 7-11 on the way to the hotel?"

"I wasn't but now I'm wishing I could."

Damn.

I forgot.

"Right," I mumbled and looked out the side window.

I heard his car roar to life and felt his hand on my knee.

"Everything's going to be okay."

I wished that was true but nothing would ever be okay again. My life would never just be mine. I would forever be watching over my shoulder waiting for the next attack, the next assault, the next time someone found me.

Since it seemed he was waiting for an answer I gave him the only one I could.

"If you say so."

Theo removed his hand from my knee and I ignored the pang of sadness. It was stupid to feel anything but appreciation for a man I would soon be saying goodbye to for the second time. The first time had been hard enough. This time was going to be brutal if I didn't stop teasing and flirting with him.

I didn't need to know this side of Theo.

I didn't need to see him smile.

He was out of the parking lot when he asked, "Tell me about Troy."

I wasn't sure if this was a trick question. If I told him about the stranger who had turned into a friend he was going to think I was one of those stupid people who didn't run when they heard the chainsaw start in a horror flick. But if I didn't explain he might not call Troy and tell him I was safely hiding somewhere new and that would be cruel.

"I met him at a truck stop," I started then decided Theo needed some backstory. "When I first got to Clarksville—that's where I was relocated to—I drove around for days making sure I knew where everything was. It was a small town so I ventured farther just in case something happened. I wanted to know what was around me. Then I thought it would be smart to make a plan, you know, just in case something happened."

Theo rolled to a stop at a red light and glanced over at me.

"That was *very* smart," he agreed.

"I found this truck stop not too far but far enough it wasn't near Clarksville and I thought if something ever happened, hitching a ride with a truck driver would be safer than hitchhiking with a rando."

"What about your car?"

"You mean the car that the Marshals gave me that I'm sure had a tracking device on it? That car?"

Since I was looking at him I unfortunately saw him smile. Thankfully it was just in profile but it was a grin nonetheless and I really didn't need to see the way the sides of his eyes creased when his lips tipped. Not even the barest sight of it in the mostly dark car. So I looked out the windshield and watched the road.

"Yeah, Bridget, that car."

"Why are you calling me Bridget again?"

"Because we're in the safety of my car and no one can hear us."

"No one followed us to Maryland. Or if they did, they've been led on a crazy ride in the last four days."

Theo checked his rearview mirror before telling me, "No one's following us now either."

Well, that was good news.

"I didn't think you liked the name Cindy," he continued.

"I like the name, but I'm not Cindy or Brenda."

"No." He chuckled. "You're not a Cindy or a Brenda."

Gah.

I needed to add that to the list of things I didn't need to know, or see, or hear.

And by the by he had a great laugh.

I shifted in my seat trying to get comfortable without scratching the soft leather.

"Relax."

There was no way I was relaxing in this car so I went on to finish my story.

"Anyway, I figured if shit hit the fan and I needed to ditch my car I'd go to the truck stop so that's what I did. Troy was there and I asked him for a ride. He was supposed to drop me off in Philly but thankfully he drove me all the way to Annapolis. But when I got here I realized all I knew was your first name and I had no way of finding you. My one screw-up in my exit plan and it was a huge one."

I heard Theo's inhale and turned to see what was wrong. At the same time he was looking over at me. For a moment our eyes locked then he dragged them back to the road and asked, "Me?"

His question was breathed out in a whoosh of air that rushed out of his chest. That one word filled the interior of the car and pressed into my chest and for some reason it felt like it was the most important question I'd ever been asked. Like my life depended on getting the answer correct.

"Yes, you."

A long heavy silence ensued and I was worried I'd failed the test.

"How did you find me?"

"Well, Troy told me his son was good with computers and could help me. And by the way did you know that there's no phone listing for Z Corps?"

"Yeah. Zane was tired of getting warranty center calls so he had Garrett erase all traces of the office number. Took G a week to scrub the internet but he did it."

Well, wasn't that handy-dandy Zane had someone to erase his phone number? If I still had a phone I'd ask him to scrub my number, too.

"How nice for him," I muttered. "Troy's son's name is Lewis. That's how I remembered Zane's last name. It was taking Lewis too long to find Zane and Troy needed to deliver his haul and he refused to leave me in Maryland until I found you so I went with him to Pittsburgh. After that he drove to Hershey where he lives and dropped off his rig and picked up his car. Once we did that we drove back down to Annapolis. Lewis had found an address for Z Corps so we went by the office but no one was there. When we went back today I saw Zane pulling out of the parking garage and we followed him. Once we saw it was a wedding I didn't want to interrupt so we waited in the parking lot."

"You've been sitting outside in the parking lot for the last three hours?"

"Yeah."

"Christ."

I didn't understand what the big deal was. Barging into someone's wedding was rude.

"Was it a nice wedding?"

"Was it a nice wedding," he repeated under his breath. "Yeah, it was a great wedding. But I could've used the save over an hour ago when my teammates started dancing like idiots."

My involuntary laughter spilled out of me before I could stop it. I couldn't imagine any of the men who had guarded me dancing.

"Did you dance?"

"Fuck no."

Well, alrighty then. I guess Theo didn't like to dance.

"I'm sorry you're missing the rest of the reception."

"Did you miss the part about me needing a save an

hour ago? Kira was inching her way over to me. It was only a matter of time before she found me hiding in the corner and dragged my ass out to the dance floor."

So maybe I didn't feel too terrible about interrupting his evening.

"Well, you're welcome then."

This time when his laugh filled the car it was more than a chuckle. It was rich and warm and it felt like a thousand butterflies had taken flight in my belly.

Theo laughing had just been moved up to the number one spot on my list of things to avoid if I wanted to keep my heart and sanity in check.

4

I WAS HANGING ON BY THE BAREST THREAD.

My control was going to snap any second and Bridget hadn't even told me about *why* she'd run. Just knowing she'd spent four days with a trucker named Troy was enough to send me over the edge. But it was her backpack sitting on a hotel bed that was inching me closer to losing my temper.

A backpack.

That was it, that was all she owned.

After everything she'd done, all that she'd given up, all of her worldly possessions fit into a small bag. And fuck me, I knew how that felt. I knew the sickening feeling of leaving everything behind.

Christ, was it hot in here or was I sweating from the exertion it took not to throw that fucking backpack out the door?

"You're worrying me," Bridget softly said.

With effort I tore my eyes off the bag and looked at Bridget sitting on the edge of the bed. Once again her hands were clasped in her lap, back straight, and more worry than there should've been blemished her beautiful face.

Thank fuck the marks around her neck Troy had mentioned had faded. My appreciation was two-fold. Most importantly the fading meant she didn't have to see the bruising when she looked in the mirror. It also meant I didn't see the worst of the damage. The last thing I wanted was Bridget getting a glimpse of the man I'd become, the man I'd been fighting to lay to rest since I'd gotten back to the States.

"I told you and I meant it, you're totally safe here. After you tell me what happened in Clarksville I'll reassess and we'll move to a safe house tomorrow if necessary."

"I'm not worried about me. I'm worried my clothes are going to catch fire from the death rays you're shooting at my bag."

It was a strain but I fought my eyes dropping back to her bag and instead kept them focused on Bridget. She looked uncomfortable, confused, and tired. None of which I could ease until I understood what had happened and how we were going to solve her problems.

"Are you ready to talk about what happened?"

The tired slid out of her gaze and she went on alert.

"Bridget, the sooner you tell—"

"I know," she interrupted me. "I'm just..." she trailed off and frowned.

"You're what?"

"I'm just over it. All of it. You know it's almost been a year?"

I did know. When Z Corps had taken over her protection detail we'd received a brief from the Marshals that gave the bare minimum. It had been Garrett who'd done a deep dive into Bridget's background and the case history. It was likely I knew more about her former employer, Raven, than she did and I was certain I knew more about the owner Mark Shillings. Though the company was now defunct and Mark was sitting his ass in federal prison for treason among the other charges he'd been found guilty of thanks to Bridget.

I didn't offer her any platitudes or insult her by telling her she'd done the right thing coming forward. I had first-hand knowledge the right thing didn't mean dick when your whole life imploded as a result.

Instead I simply told her, "I know."

"It's never going to be over, is it?"

My stomach clenched at her whispered question.

Or was it a statement?

She was likely correct that it would never be over for her. She'd be watched for the rest of her life. Instead of lying to her I said, "Let's focus on the here and now. Tell me what happened in Clarksville."

With a deep inhale she began, "I got home from the grocery store and took the bags to the kitchen. I went back to double check I locked the front door." She stopped and shook her head. "Spoiler alert, I didn't. There was a man standing in my living room. He—"

"Did you recognize him?"

Bridget shook her head again. "No."

"Do you remember what he looks like?"

"Honestly, he looked like Roger Federer."

"Who?"

"The tennis player," she told me slowly like I was dim.

"I don't watch tennis."

Bridget's head tilted to the side and her brows pulled up.

"You don't watch tennis?"

She looked absolutely scandalized with her head tilted to the side and her brows pulled up. She also looked cute as fuck—which wasn't helping *my* focus.

I refrained from explaining that for the last ten years I'd been dead, at least on paper. And during those years I'd been overseas hunting. What little downtime I had was not spent watching tennis.

"Nope."

"Seriously? He won Wimbledon eight times—"

"Babe, I hate to cut you off, but I don't know who he is."

"Right," she muttered. "Sorry."

Christ, even her pout was cute.

"No need to be sorry. Just give me the basics."

Bridget shifted on the bed, finally scooting back until just her feet were dangling off the edge.

One bed.

One bed and two uncomfortable hotel chairs. It was going to be a long, painful night.

"Brown hair, a little long on top. Brown eyes. Athletic build. Not overly tall, but tall. Strong jaw. He had on a pair of jeans, loafers, and a light blue polo shirt."

"Loafers?"

"Yep. Brown suede with those tassels in the front. And they had white stitching around the toe."

That was an interesting observation. Not particularly useful, but interesting, nonetheless.

"Any tattoos? Scars?"

"No."

Now for the hard part.

"Okay, so he was in your living room. Then what happened?"

"He pounced. I didn't have a chance to run before he had his hand around my arm. The first thing he did was slap me. I struggled but he was too strong. I couldn't get away." She paused, blinked, then narrowed her eyes. "He had spicy breath."

How in the hell was breath spicy?

"Spicy?"

"Yeah, like he was chewing cinnamon gum. I was screaming my head off and he leaned close and shouted at me to shut up. His breath was spicy. And he kept asking me what I saw."

Fucking hell.

Not that I ever thought Bridget's attack was random but her assailant asking what she saw was the confirmation I needed to put that far-fetched theory to bed.

She went on to explain the man had repeatedly asked her what she'd seen while shaking her. That was until he'd gotten her on the floor. Then he'd wrapped his mother-fucking hands around her throat and strangled her until her neighbor had come in.

Throughout her retelling of the story I stood, forcing myself not to pace. I kept my gaze steady on Bridget. There was no emotion in her voice and I wondered if at any time in the last four days she'd processed the attack. From the look of her, I had to guess no. She was still in survival mode. A tactic I was all too familiar with.

"Bridget," I started softly.

I watched as the rigidity crept up her spine until her back was straight and her shoulders tense.

"Please don't," she begged. "Whatever you're going to say next, I'm not ready to hear it."

She was likely correct but she needed to talk about what had happened to her.

"It's more about you needing to get that fear and poison out—"

"I'm not ready for that, either," she swiftly interjected.

My phone's ringing stopped me from pushing, which was probably for the best. However, I didn't welcome the interruption.

I reached into my pocket, pulled out my cell, and saw Easton's name.

Fuck.

My time was up.

"Yeah?" I answered.

"Where are you?"

I lifted my eyes to Bridget and said, "Something came up and I had to leave."

"I can't believe you bailed." Easton chuckled. "No one was going to make you dance."

He was right about that, though I didn't have to get into a ballbusting session with my teammate so I cut to the point.

"Listen, Three, I'll call you in the morning."

He was silent for a beat. Then I knew he understood the situation when Easton went from teasing to all business.

"Do you need backup?"

The correct answer would've been yes, but I wasn't ready to bring my team in yet. The moment I mentioned Bridget's name, Zane and the rest of the guys would descend. If tonight was the only night I'd have Bridget all to myself, I was taking it. Tomorrow I'd call in my location but tonight was mine.

"I'm good."

"Right," Easton clipped. "We don't go at it alone, *Two*."

Funny, we'd been going at it alone for a decade. But Easton was right—now that we worked for Z Corps the rules had changed. Zane sent his men out as a team.

"I'll call in the morning."

"Is it your brother?" he asked.

Thankfully, for once it was not my brother causing issues.

"No. It's all good. I'll call you in the morning and brief the team but I need you to keep this to yourself until then."

Easton blew out a frustrated breath.

"Only if you promise me you're not in danger."

"I'm not."

Bridget was, but still I wanted one night without my team.

"I'll wait for your call."

Easton disconnected and as I was pulling my phone away from my ear Bridget asked, "Are you going to get into trouble?"

Get into trouble? No.

Was I *in* trouble? Yes.

That was, if the definition of trouble was in over my head with a woman who was just as much off-limits now as she was when I first met her.

I watched Bridget shift again. None of the tension had left her body and I thought back to the months I'd been guarding her. At no time had she been stiff and anxious like she was right then. She'd been rightfully irritated her life had been upended, annoyed that she had to move to a new location every time she was taken in for deposition. But at no point did she look truly scared. Now she looked like she was ready to come out of her skin.

I'd already told her more than once she'd be safe with me. I reckoned telling her again wouldn't do any good so I tried a different approach.

"Tomorrow, I'll call the team in and get you settled in a safe house. But tonight—"

"I know I'm safe with you, Theo," she cut me off.

Christ, that felt good.

"Then why are you sitting so stiff you're giving yourself a backache?"

It took her a moment to understand my insinuation but when it dawned she relaxed.

"I'm just..."

I knew what she was—scared out of her mind.

And the fuck of it was, she had good reason.

"Scared," I supplied.

"Confused," she corrected, then shook her head. "Relieved, tired, anxious."

I could see how she'd be all of those things.

But still...

"It's okay to be scared," I told her.

"So what happens now?"

Good fucking question.

I'd give her that play—for now. Then I was pushing her

to talk to me about what was truly bothering her before the effects of being attacked in her own home took root and turned ugly.

"Now, you get some sleep."

There was a long stretch of silence before she admitted, "I don't know if I can sleep."

"Have you slept in the last four days?"

Bridget's lips twitched before they curved up into a smile that left me in a momentary daze.

"Is that code for I look like shit?"

I wasn't sure she *could* look like shit. Even sleep deprived and disheveled she still looked beautiful.

"No, baby, it's code for it's late and tomorrow's going to be a long day for you."

Her mouth opened to say something but she quickly closed it and stood, gazing around the small hotel room.

"Okay. Where do you want me?"

Not only was her tone all wrong—defeated and by rote —but also her gaze darted around the room as if another bed was going to magically appear.

"What were you going to say?"

Instead of answering she focused on the stupid, fucking backpack and muttered something about getting changed.

"Look at me, Bridget."

Slowly, her eyes lifted from studying her bag on the bed and fastened onto my gaze. But now that I had her attention my mind blanked. I'd forgotten everything I wanted to say. My only thought circled around a feeling—a riot of emotions that had consumed me when I'd first met her and had not lessened over the time I'd spent with her—only to blister when I watched her get loaded into an SUV and whisked away from me. A feeling I couldn't name and I'd never understood.

"Theo?"

Jesus.

I needed to sort my shit and do it fast.

"You don't need to guard yourself around me."

"What?"

"You were going to say something," I reminded her.

She didn't bother denying it but neither did she say what was on her mind.

After a moment, disappointment flared and I jerked my chin toward the bathroom.

"Sorry, but I can't leave the room. The bathroom's going—"

"I was going to say," she cut in but paused. "I was going to ask if it would be okay with you if you laid with me for a while. I don't know if I can sleep."

The area around my heart got tight and I fought to stay rooted and not pull her into my arms.

"I haven't slept in days," she finished on a whisper.

Something sharp pierced my chest. I wasn't sure if it was the fact I'd been right and she hadn't slept since her attack or if it was because she'd trusted me with the truth. There was a difference between her coming to me for help—knowing from experience I was good at my job and could keep her safe—and sharing something she very obviously didn't want to admit.

Whatever her reason for confessing, it snapped my control and a battle ensued to keep my distance. The only way I was going to win the war was for her to physically remove herself from my presence.

"Go change, Bridget."

Her head tipped ever so slightly, her eyes stayed glued to mine, and she asked, "Why do I feel like I'm being excused?"

Fuck.

I did my best to soften my tone and tried again. "Go change. Get comfortable and we'll get you some rest."

While I try to keep my hands to myself.

With a nod she picked up her backpack and headed for the bathroom.

As soon as the door clicked behind Bridget I let out a frustrated breath. Or was it an excited breath? Was this a sign? A second chance? Was this the universe's way of giving her back to me?

What the fuck was wrong with me? Second chance, the universe? If I wasn't careful I'd start believing in soulmates and fairy tales.

Unfortunately it didn't take Bridget long to change, or so I thought. The door slowly opened and a moment later Bridget came back out in the same clothes she went in with.

"What's wrong?"

"I don't have anything to wear," she mumbled dejectedly.

"Come again?"

"I don't have anything to sleep in." She paused and her gaze glided to the bed. "At least not something appropriate to wear while we share a bed."

To say my blood pressure skyrocketed would be a gross understatement.

"What *exactly* does that mean?"

It would seem I forgot Bridget had a temper that rivaled mine and when it flared, it *flared.*

"What *exactly* is your problem?"

Well, that was easy to answer.

"You've spent four days in hotels with Troy," I reminded her. "What the fuck did you wear then?"

I'd forgotten about this, too—when Bridget got pissed her whole body became involved in the discussion. Her hands came up. One pointed at me, the other she planted on her hip, her neck craned forward, and she went off on me.

"What does Troy have to do with what I wear? Do you think I would sleep in a hotel room next to a man I don't know? I mean, really, Theo, what kind of idiot do you take me for?"

Well, that's a relief.

"You mean the man you don't know that you want me to check in with?"

Some of Bridget's irritation fled.

"Troy helped me and I do trust him as much as I can trust someone I've known for four days. I can't explain it, but he genuinely cares—not like he cares about me as Bridget, but he cares that a woman was attacked and he's the kind of gentleman who wants to make sure that woman is okay. I owe it to him to give him that peace of mind. He went out of his way to help me."

Fuck, I couldn't argue that. I got the same vibe from the man.

"For the record," I began, trying to instigate damage control. "I don't think you're an idiot."

"Oh, so just a stupid, careless woman who would share a hotel room with a man she just—"

"You're not that either," I interrupted to stop her from spiraling. "I overreacted."

Bridget's shoulders jerked, her hand dropped, and her mouth twisted into a frown.

"You overreacted?"

Her question sounded more like she was muttering to herself than asking, yet I answered, "Yes. I overreacted. I should've known better."

Her frown deepened and I was at a loss. I'd apologized. Was there something else I was supposed to do?

"I don't know what to do with that," she returned.

Now I was really lost.

I hadn't had a woman in my life beyond Kira and Layla for over ten years. To say I was rusty would be a gross assessment of what I was.

"Forgive me for being a dick?" I suggested.

There was a beat of silence right before Bridget busted out laughing. And I'd swear hearing that sound again filled my chest with the same stillness it had before. It was like listening to her happiness was what I needed to quiet my mind, to put aside all the ugliness of the past decade and just be.

"I'm sorry," she sputtered. "I'm a little wound up."

A little?

The poor woman had the year from hell.

Wisely, I didn't bring that up and instead offered her a solution to her problem.

"Here," I said as I started to unbutton my white dress shirt.

It wasn't until half the buttons were undone and I was pulling the tails out of my slacks that Bridget spoke again.

"What are you doing?"

"Giving you something to sleep in."

Bridget wasn't short but neither was she tall. She'd swim in my shirt.

"I can't..."

When she didn't finish I prompted, "You can't what?"

"Sleep in your shirt."

I shrugged the shirt off and held it out.

"Why not?"

"Why...not?"

It was then I saw where her eyes were aimed. It was also then I realized my mistake. Further from that, it was very fucking unfortunate I was in dress pants and not jeans because if she didn't stop staring at my chest like she wanted to take a long, slow lick the evidence of my appreciation was going to become very obvious.

It was with that in mind I walked my shirt to her.

"Here."

"What will you wear?"

Damn, I'm an asshole.

As soon as Bridget took the shirt from my hand I stepped back.

"I'm sorry. I didn't think about you being uncomfortable with—"

"Uncomfortable?"

Good God, she was beautiful when she smiled.

"Yes, uncomfortable with me being shirtless," I clarified.

Suddenly Bridget Keller morphed into the woman I

suspected she was before she'd turned into a whistleblower and federal witness.

And when she did, it was me who was uncomfortable. Or at least I was the one who was in pain when my dick decided he really liked this version of Bridget.

"You don't make me uncomfortable, Theo."

It wasn't the words she spoke; it was the teasing way she'd delivered them. It was the smirk on her kissable lips that made an innocent statement flirtatious.

Fuck. This wasn't good. She needed time and I needed to figure out what was going on before this—whatever this was—went any further. I'd managed to push aside my feelings for her for months; I could do it again.

Maybe.

For a couple of days—at most.

5

STUPID, STUPID ME.

I'd read that all wrong, or more accurately, I'd done that all wrong.

I thought for sure Theo would understand I was flirting but the way he'd stared at me then told me to go back into the bathroom and change told a different story.

Gah. I sucked at this. Not only that but it really wasn't the right time for me to be flirting nor was it the time for me to think about how much I'd missed him when I left to go into witness protection.

I finished buttoning up his shirt, trying my best not to sniff the material like a stage-five weirdo. But when the woodsy scent filled my nose I couldn't help but to inhale deeply. That wasn't creepy, right? I was just breathing. Everyone needed to breathe. But did everyone moan when the scent filled their senses? Yeah, probably not.

I had no idea what cologne Theo wore, but whatever it was it should've been named Hero. No, it should've been called Sexy Hero. I could plan a whole branding campaign around the scent, which would include Theo's gorgeous face being on all the marketing materials. And now that I'd seen his bare chest I confirmed what I'd suspected was a tossup over which was better—his strong, chiseled features, stubbled jaw, and deep brown eyes or his strong, chiseled chest and abs with a dusting of brown hair that did wonders for highlighting his muscles. Face, chest, abs, each individually could sell the worst-smelling cologne. All together, the bottles would be flying off the shelves regardless of the scent.

Two knocks on the door pulled me from my ridiculous thoughts.

"You okay in there?" Theo called.

No, I was not okay. I was embarrassed I'd flirted. I was sort of embarrassed I'd snapped at him, though I was forgiving myself for being bitchy since I'd had a shit year and a horrible couple of days. And apparently I'd also gone crazy since I was standing in the bathroom of a hotel room thinking about ad campaigns for a make-believe cologne.

Great. Awesome.

I was a nut job.

"Yeah, I'm good!" I shouted through the door.

I blew out a breath, snatched my backpack off the counter, and opened the door. I made it no farther when I came face-to-face with Theo. Face-to-face but not eye to eye since his were cast down on what I assumed were my legs. Make that my *bare* legs. I'd checked and double checked that the shirt covered all of the important stuff; actually it fit me like a dress. Not a sexy one, but a mid-thigh loose dress that I would have no problem wearing out in public.

Then why did I feel like I was naked?

When his gaze didn't immediately lift, and with less than a foot separating us, I had an overwhelming urge to retreat. Somehow this was different from all the times Theo had seen me in shorts. Different in a way that his eyes had never lingered. He'd never stared. He'd never actually acknowledged I was a woman. I mean, he obviously knew I was a woman, but he'd always treated me like I was a client—period. But right then he was staring and when his gaze slowly lifted to mine it was like he was seeing me for the first time.

And when his hand lifted and his thumb gently skimmed the now faint bruise on the apple of my cheek I watched his eyes narrow before he dropped his hand.

"Ready?" His rumbled question took me by surprise.

Ready?

Did I miss something? I was stuck back on the way he'd looked at me, not to mention how sweetly he'd touched me. What was I supposed to be ready for?

"For what?"

"Bed."

The area between my legs screamed yes while my brain played catch up. Unfortunately when it did, I remembered I'd asked him to lie with me until I fell asleep. But it was too late—my mind had wandered in a different direction and the evidence of the sharp turn it had taken was dampening my undies.

"Sure," I squeaked out.

Theo quirked one brow.

"I mean, yeah, I'm ready," I tried again in a lower

octave that didn't make me sound like I was overeager to jump into bed with him.

When his brow didn't drop I knew I'd missed the mark by a mile.

"Are you sure you're okay? If you've changed your mind, I can take the chair."

At his offer my eyes slid to one of the two chairs by the window.

There was no way Theo was sleeping in a chair. And not just because his large frame would barely fit in one to sit, forget sleeping.

"I haven't changed my mind."

"Then what's wrong?"

"Nothing."

Gah. Why was my voice pitching high?

"Bridget—"

"I'm fine," I rushed out, needing to end this conversation. "Let's just go to bed."

As soon as the words left my mouth I felt my face heat.

Theo's hand lifted again but this time he brushed his knuckles over my cheek, a good indication that heat had manifested itself on my cheeks which was crazy embarrassing.

"You're..." he trailed off, dropped his hand, then shook his head.

"I'm what?"

Without missing a beat he said, "C'mon, you're tired."

I was pretty sure that was not what he was going to say, but unlike Theo I wasn't brave enough to push.

Theo turned and when he did I was happy he could no longer see my face. I was quite positive I wasn't hiding my reaction to the way his lats winged out and peaked in hard muscle, making a deep valley down the center of his back. A dip I wanted to trace with my tongue. Shoulders I wanted to dig my nails into, and smooth, taut skin I wanted to run my hands up and down.

If I hadn't been so stunned I might've questioned my thoughts, I might've even reprimanded myself for staring. However, I was using all of my focus to stop myself from rushing across the room and begging Theo to do all of the crude, dirty things I'd been fantasizing about since the day I'd met him.

Now *that* snapped me out of my daze.

Unluckily, I was too late and he'd stopped by the bed and shifted to look at me. Since I'd been openly gawking there was no hope of hiding it.

Maybe I shouldn't be hiding it. Maybe I should wise up and use our very limited time together to put this stupid crush to rest. Or maybe I should stop thinking about him altogether and save myself the rejection.

"Bridget," he called.

With a mental shake of my head I dislodged my inappropriate thoughts and made my way to the bed. I didn't stop when I neared him nor did he stop me from crawling onto the mattress and settling in on the farthest edge.

"You comfortable?"

The bed wasn't huge, but it was a queen-size. If I stayed on the very edge he could fit and we wouldn't touch.

But was it comfortable? No.

"Sure."

Through the silence I didn't dare to look at him, too

afraid he'd see through my lie. But Theo didn't need my gaze to know I wasn't telling the truth.

"Is there a reason you're lying to me?"

Yes, there were about ten reasons why I was lying to him. All of them revolved around the months' worth of dreams I'd had and the desire to have him get into bed next to me now in hopes that I could sleep.

"I'm not—"

"Stop," he barked.

I pressed my lips together and kept my eyes trained on the ceiling.

"Let's start again," he suggested. "Is there a reason half your body's hanging off the bed?"

Before I could think better of it I answered.

"Yes."

"And that would be?"

"To give you room."

Suddenly the bed dipped and Theo was close. So very close I was afraid to turn my head and verify his proximity. I was hauled to the center of the bed. Then he dropped to his side, twisted, and clicked off the lamp before he fell to his back.

Then there we were lying side by side in the dark.

My mind whirled in an attempt to come up with something to say while at the same time I tried to get my heart rate under control. Failing at both I started to panic and I was no less anxious when Theo's voice rumbled from beside me.

"Relax."

Relax?

Was he crazy?

"Sure."

Damn, was my voice squeaking again?

"Baby, relax."

"Just because you add a *baby* to it doesn't make it any easier."

Truth be told, him calling me baby made me want to squeeze my thighs together to relieve some of the excitement the word created.

"I have a brother," he weirdly announced.

In all the months he'd been my bodyguard he'd never told me a single personal thing. He'd listened to me tell stories about growing up in California but he'd never shared where he'd grown up. I'd blathered on about my grandmother, waxed poetic about all that she'd taught me, but I knew nothing about his family.

I wasn't entirely sure what to do with this information.

But lying there in the dark I felt like he'd given me a gift, a huge one, which was strange because telling me he had a brother wasn't exactly earth shattering. Yet it was.

"Are you close with him?" I asked.

Silence. Then he blew out a long breath.

"We used to be. He's actually my half-brother. My dad died when I was two. My mom remarried. I was five when Bronson was born."

There was no missing the pain in Theo's voice and I wasn't sure if it was because of his brother or because, like me, even though years had passed talking about a deceased parent still caused his heart to ache.

"I'm sorry about your dad," I whispered.

"I don't have memories like you do."

I had memories of my mother—a lot of really great

memories. They were both a blessing and a curse. Some days the only thing that stopped the pain was remembering the good times. But other days the memories made me miss her more. They were a reminder she was gone before she had a chance to see me graduate high school. She wasn't there for my eighth grade formal or my prom. She didn't see me off on my first date. She hadn't been there when I had my first kiss. All the firsts she'd missed. All the conversations I needed to have with her, all the questions that had gone unanswered. All the time that was lost to us.

Instead of commenting, I slid my hand closer to Theo's until they were touching. What I didn't expect was Theo to hook our pinkies together and continue with his story like he hadn't just melted my insides with the tiny gesture.

"I fucked up and now my brother won't forgive me."

"People fuck up," I told him. "Sometimes it takes time to heal the hurt and forgive."

The silence stretched on for so long that there in the dark with Theo's pinkie hooked with mine my body started to relax. I was drifting off to sleep when I thought I heard Theo whisper, "I should've stayed dead."

6

A HAND GLIDING OVER MY CHEST PULLED ME FROM sleep. A muffled moan had me fully awake and taking stock of my surroundings and the woman who had draped her body over mine. My hand was on her ass, her head rested on my shoulder, her lips were pressed to my throat, her leg rested over mine.

Another moan. This one was a wisp of air I felt across my skin. My hand cupping her ass instinctively flexed and pulled her closer. Her leg hitched higher, her knee nudged my hard cock, reminding me that not only had I not woken up next to a woman in over a decade but the only action my dick had seen in years was from my right hand. And in the last year that action was fueled by fantasies of the woman who was currently wrapped around me.

The smart thing to do would've been to gently roll Bridget off of me. The safest thing would've been for me to roll her off then get out of bed and take a cold shower. However, before I could do any of those things her lips parted and her tongue teased up the side of my neck.

"Bridget," I called.

"Mmm," she hummed. "You taste good."

Fuck.

"Wake up."

"I am," she returned before she went back to tasting my neck.

"We need to—"

"Fuck," she boldly supplied.

I was going to say get the hell out of this bed and get dressed but my suggestion died a quick death when she shifted to straddle my hips. The hard peaks of her nipples pressed against my chest through the thin material of my dress shirt while she kissed and licked her way around my neck down to my shoulder. I felt the buttons scrape my skin as she slid herself down to kiss my chest, stopping to circle my nipple before she continued her descent. My brain kicked in when her hand went to the button of my pants. My hand captured hers before she popped the button and freed my throbbing cock.

Only her eyes lifted when she said, "I want to."

My dick wanted her to, as well.

"This isn't smart," I countered.

"Why not?" she asked and pulled her hand free. "I want to," she repeated as she traced the outline of my erection. "And by the feel of this you want it, too. So what's the harm?"

The harm was once I had her there would be no going back. I wouldn't be able to watch her walk away again. I would selfishly put her in danger by insisting she refuse witness protection. Not that I hadn't already planned on fighting to keep her with me but if the risk was too great I would have no choice but to give her up to keep her safe.

Unfortunately the thought of losing her again had the opposite effect I was hoping for. It merely served as a reminder this might be our only chance—my only chance to have her.

Before I could reconcile which would be worse—never having her or having her once then watching her be stolen away from me again—Bridget rose to her knees. I watched as she unbuttoned one then two buttons. My attention became acute when she undid the third, exposing the barest hint of her breasts. By the fourth my hands came off the bed, but instead of stopping her I took over. With one hard yank the rest of the buttons gave way, revealing her perfect tits and red lace panties.

"Is that you giving me permission?" she teased.

With great effort I tore my gaze from the lace covering her pussy and found a devilish grin on her angelic lips.

Fuck it. If this was my only shot I was taking it.

"Unbutton my pants and free my cock."

That grin turned into a triumphant smile. But instead of doing what I'd instructed she started to shrug my shirt off.

"Leave the shirt on."

With a nod she went to work unbuttoning then unzipping my pants. When she reached in and pulled my cock from the confines of the material I breathed a sigh of relief.

"Commando," she muttered. "I approve."

Her grip was firm as she slid her hand up and down my shaft. Her smile was wicked when her eyes tipped downward to watch herself stroke my cock.

"Hand between your legs," I commanded.

Without hesitation her hand went to her stomach and her fingertips dipped under the lace.

"Over the panties. I want to watch your fingers circle your clit."

I expected some pushback—a questioning look at a minimum. But she followed my command and slid her hand over the lace, cupping her pussy over the fabric before she dragged her middle finger up her center and started rubbing.

"Like this?"

"Just. Like. That," I grunted and watched her toy with her clit while she jerked me off.

The sight before me had my balls drawing up. I told myself it was because I hadn't had sex in years but I knew that was a lie. It was her. It was the way her hand felt wrapped around my cock. It was her boldness. It was the way she'd yielded to my demands. It was the months of falling in love with her, then the months of missing her.

Her thumb swiped the bead of moisture leaking from the tip of my cock and smeared the liquid over the sensitive head. She asked, "Is this limited to a hand job or do I get to taste you for real?"

Fuck, she was killing me.

Killing me in the best of ways.

Ways that were going to end with her having a mouth full of my come.

"Don't stop toying with your pussy..." I got no more out before Bridget scooted down my thighs and leaned forward. My gaze zeroed in on her mouth just in time to watch her circle her tongue around the rim of my dick. Not a lick—a whisper of a tease that had me fighting for control.

Bridget's eyes tipped up, mine caught on hers, and a new kind of heat flared in my chest as her hand slowly slid down my dick, her tongue chasing her fist, her eyes flashing in triumph.

"You got two more seconds of that," I warned.

I lost her tongue on my dick when she asked.

"Of what?"

"Playtime."

"But I like—"

"Know what you'd like more?" I interrupted. "My mouth on your pussy."

Bridget's lips tipped up in a playful smirk.

"I'm not sure that's true," she countered on an upward glide of her hand.

"How about you finish sucking me off? Then we'll see who's right."

I lost sight of her sexy smile when she went back to teasing my dick. Thankfully I didn't have to wait two seconds. With one last swirl of her tongue she swallowed me whole.

"Jesus."

The word was torn from my throat as Bridget worked my cock. She didn't suck me off—the woman gorged herself on my dick, leaving me utterly helpless to do anything but enjoy the ride.

It didn't take her long before my vision swam with pleasure and my orgasm quickly approached.

"Pull off and jack me off if you don't want a mouthful."

Bridget's answer was to take me to the back of her

throat. The feel of her warm, wet mouth and the sound of her gagging and slurping proved to be too much. My muscles constricted, my jaw clenched, my control snapped, and I took over fucking up into her mouth. Seconds later, euphoria took over. I had just enough wherewithal to slow my thrusts as she attempted to swallow my climax.

"Christ," I groaned as she lapped up the last of my orgasm that had spilled from her mouth. When she was done, she sat back on her heels and smiled.

Satisfaction radiated from her in a way that meant there might be some validity to her earlier denial.

"Climb up here, Bridget. I want your pussy on my face."

Her smile died and uncertainty crept in. Yet she still slowly scooted up my legs, trepidation obvious. I waited until she was straddling my chest before my hands went to her thighs, halting her progress.

"Bridget?" I called.

"Yeah?"

"Look at me, baby."

Her head tipped down but her gaze went to the pillow.

"Eyes," I demanded and hers slid to mine. "Now, tell me why you look scared."

She did her best to infuse conviction in her lie when she answered, "I'm not scared."

"Five minutes ago, you were cocky as fuck when you wanted my dick in your mouth. Now you look like you're ready to flee."

I watched as she dragged her teeth across her swollen bottom lip. Her cheeks were tinged pink, which I wouldn't have thought possible seeing as I hadn't lied—five minutes ago the woman above me had been single-minded and bold. She hadn't had any hang-ups asking for what she wanted. Now she was blushing and hesitant.

"I've..." she started. "I don't..." she trailed off again. I gave her legs a squeeze of encouragement which she read and finished, "I've never done this."

What the fuck?

"No one's ever eaten your—"

"No. I mean, yes. I've done *that* but I've never done it this way."

Fuck yeah.

Someplace inside of me was happy to be the first to give her this.

"Then you're in for a treat."

Bridget rolled her eyes and came back to herself.

"Are you going to tell me what to do?" she sassed. "Or are you just going to lie there and torture me?"

"Oh, I'm going to torture your pussy as soon as you climb up and sit on my face."

"Sit on your face," she breathed, looking horrified.

Christ, she was cute as fuck.

But it was time to move this along.

I didn't bother with any further verbal explanation. My hands slid around to her ass and I lifted. When I had room to move I shifted down the bed quickly maneuvering her knees beside my head.

"Hold on to the headboard."

She pitched forward.

"You holding on?"

"The best I can do when the headboard is attached to the wall. Now what?"

I couldn't help my smile at the impatience in her tone.

There were some things that were better shown—this was one of those things. I moved my hands to her hips, gathered the red lace, and with a vicious tug I tore the delicate elastic and shoved the offending material to the side.

"If those weren't one of the only three pairs of panties I owned I would think that was the hottest thing that's ever happened to me."

I'd buy her a hundred pairs of lace panties tomorrow just so I could rip them off and hear that sexy rasp again.

"Closer," I demanded and pulled her down onto my awaiting mouth.

"Theo," she gasped.

My plan was to give her a little payback and tease. Draw this out and make her beg. But with one swipe against her drenched pussy I couldn't hold back.

"Ohmigod."

Another breathy gasp followed by a jolt.

Oh, yeah, this was going to be fun.

My hands spanned her hips, holding her where I wanted, and I got down to the business of turning her gasps into cries of pleasure.

I ate.

Instinct took over and she rocked her hips while my tongue speared in. Her legs trembled when I sucked her clit into my mouth. She moaned and pleaded, chasing the orgasm I wouldn't let her have.

"Theo," she groaned, sounding close. "Please."

I pulled back and traced the seam of her pussy, not giving her nearly enough to push her over the edge. If she wanted it, she was going to have to take it. Demand it.

"Dammit, Theo."

Frustration laced her tone. Her body shook with need.

"I need to come," she panted.

I bet she did.

But I wasn't giving it to her.

Not yet.

Not until she let go.

Not until I knew she was out-of-her-mind crazy.

Bridget shifted above me. A moment later I felt her fingers glide through my hair before she fisted a handful and yanked.

And there she was—my beautiful, sweet, cute, bold, fiery goddess who could balance following my orders with making her own. She knew when to submit and when to command.

Perfect.

"Finish me," she demanded.

With one last slow lick from her ass to her clit I stopped teasing and I devoured her. Savoring the taste of her excitement. Relishing the way she dripped down my chin and coated my lips. Loving the way her need had overpowered her mind and she ground down and rode my face with wild abandon.

Every sound out of her pretty mouth was beautifully filthy. But nothing was more beautiful than the way her back arched and she chanted my name as her climax hit. I slowly brought her down, licking and nibbling the inside of her thighs until the trembling stopped, her grip on my hair loosened, and I heard a long sigh of contentment.

Only then did I move her down to my chest. I took my time memorizing the way she looked perched above me, my dress shirt open and hinting at the beauty that remained hidden. The curve of her full tits a sexy tease. The smile that graced her stunning face magnificent. All of her so perfect it was hard to look at her knowing there might come a day I'd have to choose—her safety or my selfishness.

I knew what I wanted.

I knew I might not get it.

That was the crux of my issue—loving her and knowing one way or another it was going to lead to heartache. An emotion I'd easily avoided for over a decade.

"Am I crushing you?" Her question pulled me back to the present.

The shrill ringing of my phone saved me from my thoughts.

"No, baby, but I should get that."

That was when reality came crashing down around both of us.

7

I WATCHED AS THEO SAT ON THE EDGE OF THE BED, back bowed forward, elbows resting on his knees, phone up to his ear. I was only half paying attention to a conversation I knew centered around me. But now that Theo's end of the call was mostly grunts and one-word answers I stopped listening altogether. I waited for my freakout to come but it never did.

I wasn't particularly shy about sex. In the past I'd carefully selected my partners and didn't get into bed with them until some sort of trust had been built. But I'd never been comfortable enough to make demands. I was a follower. I paid attention. I wanted to please my lover. But Theo was different. I didn't want to please him, I *needed* to. From the moment I woke up wrapped around him, all the months of missing him slammed into me. The thought that this might be my only chance stole through me until a boldness grew.

This was Theo.

I trusted him more than I'd ever trusted anyone.

I'd sought him out knowing he was the only person who could save me.

I didn't regret what we'd done. I wasn't embarrassed. I wasn't ashamed. But Theo's posture worried me. He'd also said something about us having sex was not smart. I wasn't sure—no scratch that—I was positive my heart couldn't take hearing him tell me he regretted what we'd done. It was the fear of rejection that had me scrambling out of bed.

I was nearly at the bathroom door when Theo's arm hooked around my waist, pulling me to a stop. I felt his lips brush the side of my neck before he went back to his call.

"Right. Give us an hour and we'll be in." There was a pause as he listened then, "Easton knows where my go-bags are." I didn't hear him give the caller a farewell but his next statement was for me. "Shower, then we have to hit the road."

I pinched my lips and nodded.

"You okay with what happened?" he asked softly.

I debated giving him the simple answer. The one that let him off the hook without having to discuss the messy feelings that came with sex. But feeling his heat at my back, his hand on the bare skin of my hip, remembering the way his tawny eyes had heated when he watched me take his dick in my mouth, gave me the courage to tell the truth.

This was Theo.

He might reject me but he'd let me down easy.

"I'm scared you're going to tell me that was a mistake and it's never going to happen again. Or worse, you regret it."

His hand moved from my hip up along my rib cage

until he was cupping my breast, his thumb slowly grazing over my nipple.

"That's most definitely going to happen again," he growled in my ear, causing goose bumps to surface. "And the only thing I regret is being interrupted before I got the chance to fuck you."

His forefinger joined his thumb at my nipple and he rolled.

"Still scared?" he asked.

No. I was petrified.

As much as I wasn't going to waste the time I had with Theo I knew the pain of losing him. And the first time that happened he'd been nothing more than the bodyguard I'd fallen in love with. This time he'd be the man who owned my body and my heart.

This time when I got sent away it was going to kill.

"No," I murmured, leaving out the rest.

"Unfortunately we don't have much time."

I nodded again, not sure how to respond to his announcement when he was still rolling my nipple.

"I got to taste you," he strangely stated, his hand now skimming down my stomach. "But I didn't get to *feel* you."

I understood what he meant when two fingers plunged deep inside my pussy.

"Fucking hell. Hot and wet," he groaned, pumping harder. "I can't wait to get my dick here."

My head fell back against his shoulder as Theo built my pleasure at a breakneck pace.

"Tonight when we get to where we're going I'm going to take my time," he promised while those fingers continued to work magic between my legs. "I'm going to taste every inch of you and when I'm done you're going to climb on top and let me watch you fuck me. You're going to obey my every demand. You're going to entrust your beautiful body to me and let go."

"Yes," I whispered my agreement.

"I wasn't asking," he grunted as he ground the heel of his palm roughly against my clit. "I'm telling you that's what's going to happen. Now, be my sweet girl and ride my fingers. Don't stop until you come. I want you dripping down my hand, Bridget."

My body obeyed before my brain had a chance to tell it to.

"Harder," he demanded. "Grind down on my fingers and show me how you're gonna ride my dick."

I did as he asked and rocked my hips faster. Theo curled his fingers, the new angle hitting a place inside of me that I didn't know existed, and suddenly I was there.

"I'm going to come," I panted.

"Do it."

It was his rough demand that pushed me over. My compulsion to give him what he wanted should've frightened me. The way my body wanted to obey him over logical thought should've had me questioning my good sense. But right then I didn't have it in me to feel anything other than Theo. His stubble on the side of my face, his fingers fucking me hard and fast, his chest pressed against my back, the way his breath felt as he whispered over my skin.

Him.

I was safe.

My knees started to buckle as the fullness of my orgasm

hit. His other arm went around me, holding me up. My hips bucked, a moan slipped past my lips, my pussy convulsed, and a rightness I'd never felt before came over me and it had nothing to do with the ecstasy of my climax.

Being in his arms was simply *right*.

I was still shaky when Theo spun me around. His hand went to my cheek and his mouth slammed down on mine. My lips parted, his tongue surged in, and it was instantly the best kiss of my life. A few seconds later, Theo deepened the kiss and it became the best kiss in the history of kisses. The kiss was so good I whimpered when he broke it.

"Jesus," he muttered against my lips. "You can fucking *kiss*."

"It's you," I returned, knowing damn good and well I had never engaged in something so sublime.

His hand cupping my cheek gently skimmed across my face. His middle finger traced my bottom lip. My tongue followed, tasting myself there. I watched Theo's eyes flare and heat with desire. He liked that, me tasting myself. I knew I was right when his finger pushed past my lips and with a deep rumbling groan he asked, "You like that?"

I sucked his finger deeper into my mouth, thinking that said it all.

I was right.

"Yeah, my sweet girl likes it dirty."

He sounded pleased which in turn made me happy.

Then his finger was gone and he stepped back.

"Shower or I'm going to change my mind and stay here to see just how filthy I can get you."

That sounded like a much better plan than whatever we were supposed to be doing.

It suddenly hit me; I didn't ask what our plans were. Where he was taking me or where we were going later.

Maybe it made me stupid but I trusted he'd take care of me.

I WAS GOING to kill Theo.

Theo *and* Zane Lewis.

Theo for bringing me to Z Corps.

Zane for being a sarcastic dick.

"I don't remember you being such an asshole," I blurted out.

"Nice." Zane chuckled, uncaring I'd called him an asshole. "I stay up half the night and solve your problem while you're playing pet the kitty cat and you call me an asshole."

Despite my irritation I felt my cheeks heat.

"Damn, and that was just a guess," Zane muttered. "Hope you..."

"Don't," Theo cut in.

Easton barked out a laugh and through that laughter said, "I hope you covered your..."

"Nope," Theo interrupted that, too.

"Theo's no fool," Smith, another one of Theo's teammates, started. "He knows to wrap his..."

"Enough," Theo snapped.

"I don't know what's gotten into these men," Zane rejoined with a huge smile on his face. It was then I noticed for the first time he had dimples. The last time I'd been around Zane he hadn't so much as grinned—

forget smiling so big it made him look hot instead of scary.

"Thank fuck KK is on her honeymoon," Theo muttered under his breath.

"You should thank me for that, too," Zane returned. "You know she's gonna be pissed when she gets home and finds out there was trouble."

"Who's KK?" I asked.

"Kira. It was her wedding you crashed last night. She and Cooper left for the Bahamas at zero-dark-butt-crack of dawn."

That was just last night? It felt like weeks ago.

"She didn't crash Kira's wedding," Theo defended me.

"Right, she saved you from having to dance."

"As far as I could see there was no dancing. There were a bunch of shockingly uncoordinated men convulsing while music was playing."

"I'm a great fucking dancer."

My gaze ping-ponged between Theo and Easton as they bantered back and forth. Thankfully Theo got down to business.

"I still don't understand why the feds called you last night." Theo tapped the conference room table in front of him.

Unfortunately this brought my attention to his long, thick fingers.

Fingers that just an hour ago proved to hold some sort of sorcery.

"You mean why did Deputy Johnson from the US Marshal Service call me at midnight to tell me they lost contact with Bridget and wanted us in on the search? Is that the question or are you asking why they waited four days to bring us in? I don't know the answer to either of those but now I understand why I didn't get a call from you telling me you're in possession of a federal asset."

Possession of a federal asset.

Like I was an object, not a person.

I was so over being treated like a thing that people could control and tell what to do. It made me regret my decision to help the government more. I should've said no and walked away. If I had I would still have my life.

But good men and women could've died.

Government secrets would've been sold.

I never would've been able to live with myself. So really I would've been as miserable as I was now, only I'd also have guilt weighing heavy on my conscience.

"I'm not a federal asset and I found Theo and asked him for help," I cut in.

"And you think that makes it better?"

"No, what I think it makes it is none of the Marshals' business. I gave them a shot at protecting me and they failed. I was found. I no longer want their services."

"You want Theo's services?"

I wanted Theo, period, but I wasn't going to tell the asshole Zane Lewis that.

"I want to stay alive and the only person I trust to keep me that way is Theo."

"Bummer," he weirdly mumbled.

"You'd rather I die?"

I couldn't keep the hurt from my voice. I didn't imagine I was someone Zane would say he liked and I was sure there were times I'd been a pain in his ass while he was having his men guard me before I testified, but I was nowhere near bitchy enough for him to consider me expendable.

"Fuck no."

"He's just salty because he won't be able to give Theo shit," Easton explained.

Why would Zane want to give Theo shit?

"No," Smith contradicted. "He's salty because his sidekick is going to be gone a week and he'll have no one to laugh at his stupid jokes *and* he won't be able to give Theo shit because he's already made up his mind and so has Bridget."

I turned my head to see Theo's reaction to the conversation going on around us. I'd expected frustration but instead he was smiling.

"What can I say? I'm smarter than the rest."

"That's what they all say right before they come crying to me asking how to keep the woman they were too dumb to hold close," Zane snarked.

Some of Theo's smile faded.

"Never been accused of being dumb, boss," Theo remarked.

"No, but that mountain of misplaced guilt will be your downfall."

Zane's words caused an immediate reaction from Theo. The temperature in the room seemed to plummet. I wouldn't have been surprised if the windows frosted over with the icy stare Theo aimed Zane's way.

"Don't," Theo spat.

"Sorry I'm late," a new voice sounded from the door.

When I turned to the newcomer I vaguely recognized him.

"Bridget, this is Garrett," Theo introduced us. "He's our information specialist."

"Hey, Bridget, nice to see you again."

"You came to the safe house to deliver my prep."

I'd only met Garrett once. He'd stopped by with a stack of testimony prep from the state attorney's office. He was only there for a few minutes and had said nothing to me but had pulled Theo into the garage to speak to him in private before he left, using the side door in the garage. At no point during that exchange did Garrett look friendly. A far cry from the smiling man who'd just said hello.

"Yep, that was me," he confirmed and placed a folder in front of Zane.

"Did you find anything?" Zane inquired.

"I found a lot. And the more I dug the less sense it made."

Zane sighed and opened the file.

"Just once I'd like a case to come across this table that's straightforward and not full of bullshit I have to wade through to find a hint of the truth."

"Bullshit," Garrett tossed back. "You'd be bored to tears."

Zane's grin clearly communicated Garrett was correct. I knew that feeling well—not the part about cases but the bored-to-tears part. WITSEC wasn't all it was cracked up to be especially when you had to leave behind the job you loved.

"Before we go over what I found I think we should go over Bridget's attack."

This was the part I was dreading.

I didn't want to relive that day.

"I already told Theo," I explained to Garrett.

"I can imagine this is hard for you but the rest of us need to hear it direct from you."

Theo had kept close to me since we left the hotel. At first it made sense; someone had tried to strangle me to death so I figured he was being cautious. But he remained close to my side when we were safely inside the Z Corps office. And when we'd all sat around the conference room table he'd scooted his chair close to mine. Throughout all of that he had not touched me—until now. I felt his pinkie hook around mine and give it a shake. I glanced to my left to find him staring at me.

"If you need time, take it. There's no rush," he gently told me.

It wasn't his soft command to take my time that bolstered my confidence. It was his nearness, the sweet gesture, the calmness in his tone.

I could do this.

I could relive the attack one more time then shove it to the back of my mind and never think about it again.

With a deep breath I retold my story. This time I remembered something I must've blocked out when the pain of my attacker's blows got to be too much.

"He's got a mark on his neck."

"You didn't tell me that."

I glanced back at Theo and explained. "I didn't remember it until now. The pain was so overwhelming I was trying to do Lamaze exercises and breathe through the pain. I totally forgot about the mark."

"Lamaze? You don't have children." Zane noted with authority yet still flipped through the file in front of him.

"I went to birthing classes with a friend back home. Her husband was a firefighter and she was sure he'd be on a call-out when she went into labor so I was her backup plan."

"What kind of mark?"

I was grateful for Easton's question. Over the months I'd done my best not to think about the friends I'd left behind. Not that it worked.

"Bridget?" Theo gently called.

Shit.

"Um, I don't know. It was mostly under the collar of his shirt. A big mole or a birthmark maybe. It didn't look like a tattoo. It was raised and a brownish black color."

Easton nodded and jotted something down on a pad in front of him.

"A birthmark?"

Garrett's question had me glancing his way.

"Or a mole."

"And no accent?"

"No. He sounded American. Not Southern or Mid-Western or Northerner. Just boring ol' American."

"Right."

I knew Garrett was done with his questions when he opened his laptop and the big screen on the wall came on displaying what looked like his desktop. I found I was right when I watched the cursor move around and a file was clicked open.

He found the file he wanted and opened that as well.

A familiar map of the Mojave Desert popped up.

"This was the first test site for the Sparrow, correct?"

The Sparrow was the smallest UAV that Raven had produced. It was a micro-drone still in the early prototype phase. By the time Mark had been arrested the Sparrow still hadn't been ready to market.

"Correct. The first tests were done there, then we moved East to the Dead Man's Wilderness Area."

"Why the move?" Easton joined.

"We were testing different terrain. Maneuverability of the UAV."

Garrett switched maps and my stomach did a somersault.

Clifton, Arizona.

A beautiful small town I never wanted to see again.

The place where my life had imploded.

"Why the move to Clifton?" Garrett continued his interrogation.

"Have you ever been to the Mojave Desert or the surrounding areas?"

"No."

"Right, well to say it is hot would be a gross understatement. More like it's the closest you'll get to hell without actually going to the bad place. You sweat and not just in the normal places, in *all* the places. Your fingertips sweat. Five minutes outside and it feels like your skin is melting off. Zero out of ten stars, do not recommend visiting unless you're feeling the need for a body detox to sweat out the demons. And even then I'd tell you to keep the demons and save your epidermis. The heat advisories were insane and meant we could only test for a few hours a day. Not to mention the Sparrow was continuously overheating."

I had never been so happy in my life as the day Mark announced he was moving the team to Eastern Arizona.

My happiness was short-lived.

"When you were in Clifton, did you ever test near the mine?"

"Mine?"

"The largest copper mine in the US is just outside of Clifton," Garrett unnecessarily told me.

You couldn't be in Clifton for more than five minutes without knowing about the copper mine. It was the largest employer in the county and surrounding counties.

"I know the mine and no, we never tested anywhere near it."

A strange look came over Garrett, one that stated plain he didn't believe me.

"Did you know that Mark had been in contact with Kathy Cobb?"

Before I could tell Garrett I had no idea who Kathy Cobb was, Theo cut in. "Where are you going with this, One?"

Theo's harsh tone drew my attention to him.

His scowl had my pinkie in his tightening.

His posture made me scramble to answer Garrett and move this along.

"I've never heard that name before. Who is she?"

"Senior vice president of operations for Dusk Mining Company."

"Why would Mark be in contact with anyone from the mining company?"

Garrett changed the image on the screen to a newspaper article dated from a year ago. The headline read: Local man still missing. Police have no leads.

The picture accompanying the article showed a man wearing a hardhat and a polo shirt with the Dusk Mining Company logo on it. The man was also smiling huge like he was proud to work at the mine.

"This is Jeff Goetz," Garrett informed me instead of answering my question.

"I don't know who that is."

"He worked at the mine before he went missing."

I was lost.

I had no idea what the mine or these people had to do with me.

"What's the connection to Shillings?" Easton asked.

"He was blackmailing Dusk Mining Company."

Now I was really lost.

"This Jeff guy was blackmailing—"

"No, Mark was."

I glanced at Zane and declared, "I'm with you."

"Come again?"

"I wish this was straightforward and not full of bullshit. I still don't understand what any of this has to do with me."

It was then Garrett dropped the bomb.

"Drone footage captured a fight. Three men on DMC property. One man pulled out a gun. One man dropped. Kathy Cobb can be seen in the footage as two men dragged the dead body away."

Drone footage.

Shit.

8

"I DIDN'T TAKE THAT FOOTAGE. I NEVER PILOTED ANY drones near the mine," Bridget rushed out.

The vehemence of her answer didn't surprise me. It was her trembling hands that grabbed my attention.

Before I could explain that no one was accusing her of participating in Mark Shillings' blackmail scheme, Garrett beat me to it.

"I believe you. But someone took that footage. Who else on your team knew how to fly the drones?"

Bridget's nose scrunched and some of the trembling subsided, but the tension in her shoulders was still visible.

"Everyone."

At some point Zane had passed Garrett's report to Easton who had spread the pages out in front of him.

"How'd you find all of this in less than eight hours?" Easton asked what I was thinking.

Garrett was good, but finding out Mark Shillings had been blackmailing the senior VP of Dusk Mining

Company and finding the evidence of that, something I would think the feds would've loved to add to the lists of his offenses—though treason carries a stiff penalty—every charge helps make a case. Which meant the feds missed the blackmail and Garrett had found it in the space of hours. That was next-level good.

"I've found that people in power who think they are untouchable are sloppy. That and Mark was just plain stupid."

"Actually, he was extremely intelligent," Bridget interjected.

"Right. Which made him stupid," Garrett pushed. "It took me less than an hour to find the account he used to email Kathy Cobbs. Want to know why?" Garrett paused for a moment but didn't let Bridget answer. "Because Mark Shillings is the kind of man who thinks he's smarter than everyone else. His intelligence makes him arrogant. He thought he could outplay the CIA and get a double dip. And there was his mistake. If he'd planned on taking his micro-drone to market he never should've taken the CIA's contract. But he thought he could have the CIA pay for the research and development *and* sell the finished drone to foreign rebels. Another oversight on his part that was shadowed by his intelligence—he thought he could handle a fucking warlord with no understanding of political climate or loyalties. He thought because Amani was a rebel he was stupid. If Mark had done the barest research on Amani Carver he would've known that the man was Harvard educated and went to boarding school in Europe and graduated head of his class. But all Mark saw was an Egyptian, stereotyped the fuck out of him, underestimated him, and got fucked because he's too stupid to realize that just because you have a high IQ doesn't actually mean you're smart."

Garrett was spot on with his assessment of Mark Shillings.

His biggest mistake was approaching the CIA to fund the development of a micro-drone that had the capability to carry a payload. Of course to cover their ass the contract didn't disclose what that payload was, however, it didn't take someone of Mark's or Amani's intelligence to suss out why the CIA would be interested in a near-silent micro-drone that had the potential to fly low to the ground and drop chemical agents. It would make a warlord especially interested if he could fly a drone over a village and drop sarin or another nerve agent and kill hundreds of people from ten miles away.

That was what the Sparrow was designed for.

Chemical warfare from a distance.

"I told you it wouldn't be boring!" a child's voice yelled from under the table.

"Shh," a second voice shushed.

What the fuck?

"Linc!" Zane bellowed. "Come get your semen demons. They're under the table again."

"Uncle," one of the boys whined.

"I told you to be quiet," the other one hissed.

Easton had already pushed back from the table and was bent at the waist looking under the table at Asher and Robbie.

"Learn anything interesting?" Easton chuckled.

"Just that smart people are stupid. And three F-words," one of the boys said.

"I'm gonna kick your dad's A-word if you keep sneaking under my table," Zane groused.

However Zane's smile contradicted his statement. He looked almost proud the boys had evaded detection for so long.

"Boys!" Linc snapped when he appeared in the doorway.

Bridget jolted at Linc's loud boom and leaned closer to me.

Two boys crawled out from under the table and simultaneously jumped to their feet.

"Did you teach them synchronized jumping or is that a twin thing?" Easton commented.

"It's a they know they're in trouble so they're trying to be cute thing," Linc shot back, then looked at his boys. "You're supposed to stay in your mom's office."

"We got bored," Asher proclaimed. "And the Kid Genius isn't here and we promised we'd tell her everything she missed when she got back. Which means we can't miss anything."

Kid Genius was Kira Cain's nickname and it was fitting. The woman was a genius when it came to computers. Her skills rivaled Garrett's. Together they were unstoppable. And she was younger than the rest of the team so she was a kid to us. A kid who had run our intel for ten years, a baby sister we all loved and adored, a kid who had grown into a strong, resilient woman who we all trusted with our lives.

"Where's your mother?" Linc asked.

"She went downstairs to the gun room," Robbie answered.

That sounded like Jasmin Parker, Lincoln's wife. The woman was the only operator on the team. I had never been out in the field with her. However her reputation preceded her. Everyone in the business knew not to fuck with Jasmin and this was before she married Zane's brother. She was a badass in her own right and wouldn't hesitate to literally gut a man if the necessity were to arise.

"Do you want children?" Zane asked Bridget.

"Um," she stammered and sat up straight. "I did. But now that I'm dead I'm not sure that's a good idea."

"Hey, that's cool!" Asher exclaimed. "I've never met a dead person before. What's it like?"

"Not fun," Bridget answered woodenly.

"I wouldn't know," Easton commented. "Theo was the only dead one on our team and he seemed to have plenty of fun."

Bridget slowly turned to look at me. Her eyes were wide and there was a shadow of hurt on her features.

"You were dead?"

Fucking hell. I was going to kill Easton.

"For ten years. Well, more like eleven."

"You didn't tell me," she accused.

No, I hadn't gotten around to telling her that I'd faked my death because that would lead to a conversation about my family, which would end with her putting two and two together about why my brother hated me. Then like the rest of my friends, she would tell me it wasn't my fault and Bronson would one day forgive me.

And I wasn't sure I deserved or wanted his forgiveness.

I'd purposefully and willfully lied.

I knew what my "death" would do to my family and yet I still went along with the plan.

Bronson was entitled to hate me for the rest of his life.

"It's complicated."

That was a total cop-out. And unsurprisingly, Bridget called me out on it.

"Right. Complicated. Like going undercover for the CIA, collecting evidence that my boss was selling information and blueprints to a warlord, being taken into protective custody for months before testifying, then faking my death and assuming a new identity. All of that plus giving up all of my personal belongings and the job I loved. Complicated like that?"

Fucking shit. I stepped into a huge pile of dog shit.

"Yes, baby, complicated like that."

"Don't *baby* me, Theo."

"New rule," Zane grunted, saving me from having to reply. "No more coming back to life. Die and stay dead. The paperwork to undead someone takes for-fucking-ever and it always causes problems. And while we're at it, no losing your memory, I won't help you find it. Been there done that and that's a pain in my ass, too."

"That's four F-words," Robbie proudly announced.

"Maybe can we try not to cuss in front of my boys?" Linc complained.

"I'm sorry, brother, are you talking to me? You do know your wife has a mouth on her and it spews more obscenities than the USS Nimitz hears in a year and she can manage that feat in half a day."

"We're working on that."

"Momma's up to twenty-five today," Asher ratted his mother out.

"Terrific."

"You said two C-words today," Robbie helpfully put in.

"I want my twenty back."

"Why? I didn't tell Momma."

The room was silent for a split second before it erupted into laughter. That was, everyone but Linc laughed. He was too busy staring at his son, waiting for him to return the hush money he'd paid him.

"On that note," Garrett started. "I already sent my files and report to everyone. The safe house in Monroe is ready for you. Easton, you're following them, right?"

"Yup," Easton answered, then looked over at me. "Your bags are in your office."

"Smith, I need you and Cash to take the meet with Johnson and his team," Zane ordered.

My gaze skidded to Smith who had an uncanny ability to become invisible even when he was sitting out in the open, or in this case at the table. His preferred method of business was silence. He was watchful, and when strategy was being discussed he never said a word unless he found a flaw in the plan, but he never participated in the planning. He was too busy finding fault and holes.

"Copy that, boss."

"That's it?" Bridget asked and I looked back at her.

"Is what it?"

"You're going to give me back?"

"Give you back?"

"To the Marshals. You're going to turn me—"

"Fuck no!"

"That's five."

I ignored Robbie and turned Bridget's chair so she was facing me.

"You and I are going to a safe house in Virginia. Easton's going to follow us as backup. Smith and Cash are going to meet with the Marshals to tell them we haven't seen you; our caseload is such we can't assist them, and wish them good luck. Then later when we're settled we're going to read over Garrett's report, which will undoubtedly include images of every employee that works at the mine, and see if you recognize any of them. While you're looking at pictures Easton and I will be looking into Jeff Goetz and why he was killed."

Once I was done explaining the plan, Bridget looked relieved. The look only served to piss me off.

"Seriously?" I snapped.

"Seriously what?" she bit back with the same venom.

"You thought I was going to turn you over the Marshals? What the fuck?"

There was a beat of silence. Shockingly, Robbie didn't fill it with his F-word commentary.

"No, I—"

"Yes, you did," I cut her off.

"Fine. I was scared for a second, okay? This is a lot to take in. I still don't completely understand what's happening or why someone would attack me or how they even found me. Cut me some slack, Theo. It's not every day I go on the lam from WITSEC."

She was right, I should've cut her a break. But the ache

in my chest at her distrust had caused hurt like a motherfucker.

"Oh, goodie, their first lovers' spat," Zane snarked. "Advice—she's right, you're wrong, admit it, move on, the end."

There were days I found it hard to believe that one of the men from Red, Gold, or Blue Teams hadn't cut out our boss's tongue. Or at least duct taped his mouth closed. Though murdering him would've been a better option—the duct tape would only piss him off, then he'd murder you before he bothered to untape his mouth.

"I'm sorry. I trust you. That's why I found you."

And just like that, my anger ebbed and so did the hurt.

"You're fucked, brother," Smith mumbled.

He wasn't wrong. I was fucked in the best kind of way.

"Let's hit the road," Easton suggested.

"Keys to the SUV are on your desk."

"Great," I sighed.

"Oh, I'm sorry. Does an Escalade not fit your standards, oh holy one?"

Zane's sarcasm was ratcheting up. It was time to leave.

"It's no M8 but it'll do," I returned and stood, holding out my hand for Bridget.

"I need to reconsider your compensation contract if you can afford a hundred-thousand-dollar luxury ride."

"I took a pay cut coming to work for you," I returned and pulled Bridget to her feet. "Being dead for a decade was a good retirement plan. Cash coming in monthly with nothing to spend it on."

"A hundred thousand dollars?" Bridget whispered.

"A hundred and thirty thousand," I corrected.

I smiled when her eyes rounded. "Ready?"

"I'm never getting in that car again."

She sure as fuck was. But I wasn't going to give Zane the pleasure of listening to another lovers' spat when I explained that her ass was going to be in my car, and often.

9

"Do you want to play Would You Rather?" Theo asked.

I turned my attention from trying to catch a glimpse of Washington D.C. from the Woodrow Wilson Bridge to Theo driving.

God, he was handsome. With a few days' worth of stubble on his jaw he was outright gorgeous. My gaze dropped to his right arm resting on the center console down to his hand then to his fingers and my mind cast back to this morning.

Long, thick, beautiful fingers...

"Bridget?"

"Huh?"

"Would You Rather. The game. You give two options and you have to pick which option you'd rather do."

Oh.

Right.

The game.

We were thirty minutes into our drive, two and a half hours to go. A game wouldn't hurt and it would help keep my mind from spiraling out of control thinking about everything Garrett had said. I still couldn't believe Mark was blackmailing someone. No, actually, I could believe it. What I couldn't believe was that no one else had found that information. As Garrett had pointed out, Mark thought he was the smartest person in the room, which made him careless.

"Do you think the government knew Mark was blackmailing Kathy Cobbs and that's why they offered me witness protection?"

"What?"

"Mark's in prison and he'll be there a long time. I testified for the government so they're not after me. Do you think they knew he was blackmailing that woman and that's why they're hiding me?"

There was a moment of silence before Theo glanced over at me before he looked back to the road and said, "I never asked, but did they explain the case in its entirety to you?"

I wasn't sure if I was offended that Theo thought I'd agree to go into witness protection without fully understanding the reasons.

"Yeah, of course."

"Right, so they explained that the evidence you got for the FBI, which was really the CIA asking the feds to run the case since the deed was being done on US soil—but make no mistake it was the CIA who was behind the whole thing—"

"How do you know that?"

"Trust me, I'm right," he bit out.

I did trust Theo, but I still wanted to know why his tone went funny when he mentioned the CIA.

"I take it you're not a fan of the CIA?" I hesitated to ask.

"You could say that."

I waited for him to say more but he didn't. And I wasn't sure pressing the topic while on a road trip was exactly smart so I let it go and told him, "They explained the evidence I gathered was enough for them to get an arrest warrant and my testimony would put Mark in prison and stop the project."

"And they explained fully that Mark Shillings had investors—some of those investors are not on the up-and-up. They weren't pleased when Raven collapsed and they're the type of men who wouldn't place blame on the man who actually fucked up—though I'd guess Mark won't be living out his sentence. They'll find a way to take him out in prison."

"Wait," I interrupted. "What does 'not on the up-and-up' mean?"

"Are you fucking shitting me?" Theo scarily whispered. "Two of Mark's investors have ties to the mob."

Wait.

What?

"Are you..." I started then stopped because I didn't know what to say. "Do you think that's who's after me?"

"No. I think Garrett's on the right track. This has to do with Kathy Cobbs."

"Are you sure?" I wheezed, finding it hard to breathe.

I had not been told that Mark had ties to the mob.

"It fucks me to have to explain this to you but if an enforcer from the mob found you they wouldn't have asked what you saw. They would've quietly killed you and walked away. Now, someone working for Kathy would want to know what you saw in an effort to ascertain if there was another risk."

Okay, that made sense but I still didn't feel any better seeing as I'd just learned that I was offered WITSEC to keep me safe from the freaking mob and not Mark Shillings wanting retribution.

How stupid was I?

"Bridget?" Theo gently called. "They played you. That's what the CIA does. They use innocent men and women to get what they need and keep them in the dark while doing it. On some level that's necessary for operational security. But in your case, they flat-out lied so you'd do their bidding, not caring you didn't fully understand what you were getting yourself into. Mark poses no real danger to you. It's the men who funded his startup that are dangerous. It's Amani Carver who is dangerous. There's a risk they'd want to find the person who shut down the operation. Amani thought he was getting the latest and greatest in new micro-drone technology to assist in his crusade to pillage and conquer and it's the investors who thought they were coming into a windfall."

Great.

A warlord and mobsters.

I wasn't sure who was scarier.

"I think I want to play Would You Rather now," I told him and looked out the side window.

"You didn't—"

"Ask the right questions," I interrupted. "Ask for an attorney to represent my interests. No, I didn't do either of those things. I was told about the nerve gas and why Mark was so hellbent on getting the proper balance for the battery life to carry a payload and they had me. They told me about the untold deaths that would occur if Mark finalized Sparrow so I jumped at the chance to stop him. And they had pictures of what nerve gas does to humans and animals before it kills them." I rushed out the last part, not wanting to remember the horrific images of flesh peeling off of children.

"Of course they did," he seethed. "They weren't fucking around. You were their only hope. The project was almost complete and they needed an insider who was already trusted. Sending someone in undercover would've taken months and they didn't have that kind of time."

Theo was right about that. Mark was getting close to solving his battery life problem. The Sparrow's flight times with a payload were getting better and better with each new prototype he engineered.

"I don't want to talk about this anymore."

"I'll drop the subject if you tell me you believe me."

"I believe you."

I heard Theo sigh and kept staring out the window, seeing nothing but boring office buildings. If D.C. proper could be seen from the Capital Beltway, I'd missed my chance.

"I didn't get to tell you what I want you to believe."

"Whatever you want me to believe, I believe. Unless you want to explain to me why you seem to hate the CIA, I think we should play the game."

There was no hesitation when he told me, "I worked for the CIA before I died. I know what kind of assholes they are because I used to be one of them."

The way Theo rapped out the words startled a laugh from me. I wasn't sure if it was the absurdity of the 'before I died' statement or if it was the way he said it that made it sound like a throwaway comment—widely used, thus normal—when it absolutely wasn't.

When I got myself under control I looked over and asked, "How'd *you* die?"

"Plane crash. You?"

Yeah, this had to be the craziest conversation I'd ever had in my life.

"You don't know?"

I watched as he shook his head. "I didn't read the report."

"Why not?"

Since I was staring at Theo I saw him clench his jaw several times before he relaxed and answered.

"Because I didn't want to know the lie. I wanted to keep the memory of you real and untarnished."

His words flowed over me, heating me from the inside out, making my stomach feel funny as my heart thumped in my chest.

"What?" I breathed.

I'd heard him—oh, boy, had I. But I needed verification he'd meant what I thought he did. A man didn't want to keep the memory of a woman real unless he cared about that woman, right?

"I knew they were taking you away from me and in doing so taking your life. I didn't want any part in that even if it was for your protection."

Taking you away from me.

Oh, yeah, he meant what I thought he meant.

"I died in a car accident," I told him. "As you know, all my family's gone. So my emergency contact was my friend Brit. She was the one notified. Obviously I don't know anything beyond that except all of my stuff was disposed of."

"Brit, the one you went to Lamaze classes with?" he asked.

"Yeah."

"Did you get to meet the baby?"

That was sweet.

"Yeah. They had a boy, named him Oscar. Don't laugh; it's a family name and she's sworn to stab the first person who calls him Oscar the Grouch."

"Right."

Theo didn't laugh but he smiled.

"He'd be one now going on two now."

Then since he was being forthcoming, or maybe because I no longer wanted to think about Brit, Jon, and Oscar and that I'd missed out and would continue to miss out—not to mention the guilt I felt for lying to my friend—I asked, "Will you tell me about your brother?"

Nothing.

No reaction at all, not even the tightening of his jaw. It was like he hadn't heard me but I knew he had.

"Maybe later," I mumbled and looked back out the window.

Minutes passed while I watched brake lights in front of us before he finally spoke.

"We were close," he started and I gave him my attention. "Brothers. Not half-brothers, not siblings, close like best friends even though I was five years older than him. There had never been a time we weren't together. Bronson's funny, and not in a way where he was trying to impress a bunch of older guys, like doing stupid shit for attention, he's just funny. So none of my friends cared when he tagged along. He's the only one I told when I applied to work at the CIA."

There was another pause. This one wasn't as long but the silence that lingered felt painful.

"It took almost nine months for interviews and background checks before I was hired. He was living in Montreal at the time, so I flew up there to tell him in person. He took me out to celebrate that night. He called it my last night being a free man. At the time I laughed at his antics but he wasn't wrong. It was also the last we spoke of it. From then on he stuck to my cover; I worked in textiles and traveled a lot. Never told a soul, not even our parents after I died. He kept my secret; he always kept my secrets. Then I fucked him over."

I wouldn't call what Theo did fucking his brother over. But I did understand the crushing remorse that went along with faking your death.

"You didn't—"

"Trust me, I did. My actions fucked him over. He could've been..." Theo paused, shook his head, and changed gears. "I lied to him. Hell, I lied to everyone. I think when I came home, my mother was so relieved she couldn't allow herself to be angry at me. But one day that relief will wear off and the pain of my lies will overtake any joy my rebirth has brought her. My stepdad is a great man—gentle, kind, forgiving. He heard me out and understands why I did what I did and respects my decision to keep the specifics from my mother. She knows what she needs to know but she never needs to know the extent of my life when I was dead. And that's what I was—I was a walking, talking, breathing dead man who had disconnected fully from the man I was before I died."

"Did your brother hear you out?"

That got me a jaw clench.

"No. He took one look at me and wanted nothing to do with me. I tried talking to him and he got in his car and drove away. I call, he hangs up. I text, he doesn't return the messages. I get it."

"Maybe—"

"No! He gets to feel what he feels. Forgiveness is his to give, not mine to take. I don't get to force my story on him to make myself feel better. I tried. I've done all I can do. I've missed my brother for over a decade now. I earned that pain. And if I go to my grave never speaking to him again, I earned that, too. I'm the one who is in the wrong here."

I didn't want to believe that.

I wanted to argue because I was in the same position and if the day came and I could come back to life and see Brit again I wanted to believe I had a chance at earning her forgiveness and friendship back.

"That's why you said you should've stayed dead."

"You heard that?"

Yep, I'd been right. I hadn't imagined his admission as I was drifting off to sleep.

He'd said it and that got me wondering.

"Did you mean it? Do you wish you would've stayed dead?"

Theo checked the rearview mirror before answering.

"Yes and no."

Well, that was clear as mud.

"Explain the 'no' part," I asked.

I figured I understood yes.

"If I'd stayed dead, I wouldn't've been at Kira's wedding. If I hadn't come back with my team I would've missed Layla finding Kevin and falling in love with him. I would've missed out on Easton, Cash, Smith, and Jonas reconnecting with Garrett and healing a bond that never should've been broken. I can't imagine my life without my team. For ten years we had a mission, we were dedicated to each other and to the cause. I wasn't willing to give them up. Which says something, don't you think? How easily I left behind my flesh and blood brother but I couldn't give up my new brothers."

Ah.

There it was.

That was why he thought he deserved his brother's eternal wrath.

"I don't believe faking your death was an easy decision."

"You're wrong. It was a no brainer. It was the only way to keep my family safe."

I wasn't going to point out the obvious—the sacrifice

he'd made. Instead I thought about what he'd said about his team. I didn't share the same bond with the team I'd worked with as he shared with his. We were all friendly, we had a good time working together, we'd gotten into some pretty heated debates about the functionality of the Sparrow but they never turned into ugly fights.

My team.

"If this Kathy Cobbs woman is behind my attack and she's trying to ascertain if there's more evidence of her involvement with that man's death wouldn't she go after Phil, Mike, and Sarah?"

"Fuck," he bit out and reached for his phone.

All the good feelings I was having about Theo opening up and sharing about his life went up in a puff of smoke.

Or more like a fireball of doom.

I WAS DOING my best to ignore the worry that had taken root in my belly by studying the contents of the pantry.

The last of the drive was spent with Theo making and receiving phone calls. He'd updated me between calls; however those updates gave me nothing beyond *Garrett's looking into it.*

Well, Garrett needed to work faster because my stomach was doing somersaults and I was starting to get queasy.

That wasn't fair. I had no doubt Garrett was working as fast as he could. He had found the root of my problem in less than half a day and the half of the day he figured it out it was the middle of the night to the wee hours of the morning. The man had to sleep sometime.

I closed the door to the pantry, getting a sense of déjà vu. For some reason every time I was moved to a new safe house the first thing I did was check the kitchen. Specifically, I'd check what food was stocked in the house. I had no idea why I did it, and as soon as we'd walked into this safe house I beelined to the kitchen.

Fully stocked.

It was weird.

If someone didn't know this was a safe house and they looked in the cabinets and fridge they'd think it was a normal family home.

Though it was far from normal. It was a hideout. A place Z Corps could stash people like me.

For the last year my life had been in a constant state of upheaval. One hit after another had kept me off balance. It had been so long I'd forgotten what normal felt like. And if the last week was anything to go by, any hope of normal in the future might never happen.

All because I took a job at Raven.

A job I was excited to get.

My dream job.

I wondered if working for the CIA had been Theo's dream, too.

Fuck dreams.

If this was how they ended I never wanted to dream another dream. I never wanted to hope for something special ever again. What was the point of working for something so hard then have it end in disaster?

I should've stayed where I was at, flying drones

checking powerlines. I liked it okay but was bored to tears. I thought Raven was my ticket to something exciting, something I could be proud of.

Turns out it was the worst decision of my life.

My biggest regret.

A regret that just might kill me.

10

Bridget was going out of her mind.

The Slurpee and KFC fried chicken I had Easton pick up on his way to the safe house had only gone so far. And that gesture had worn off about thirty minutes ago and now she was back to pacing the living room.

"Bridget?" I grabbed her arm as she passed me for the third time. "Let's go over the pictures Garrett sent over."

"Yeah, okay," she mumbled miserably.

"I know it's killing you but Garrett's working on it."

"I know."

She hadn't moved. I was still holding onto her arm. I slid my hand down and threaded our fingers together and shoved my chair away from the table. When there was enough space I gave her hand a yank and pulled her down to my lap. Not that I had to pull hard—she was more than willing to sit and rest her head on my shoulder.

I let the feel of her settle over me, the sense of rightness at her nearness, before I continued, "If you know, then why are you pacing?"

"Because I can't stop thinking that Phil has kids."

Fuck.

Mike was married, had been for a long time but for whatever reason they didn't have children. Sarah was young and single. Phil was divorced and the only person on her team who had children.

And he was the only person unaccounted for.

Garrett had easily found Sarah through her social media account, which meant someone who was looking to do her harm could find her, too. It had taken time for Garrett to find a contact to seek her out in person to explain the situation to her. He'd started with her for obvious reasons—a young, single woman who put her life on the internet was an easy target. He'd located Mike and sent Cash to Maine to offer protection. Phil however had no online presence, no wife who posted on Instagram. He wasn't answering his cell and no calls had been made from his phone in four days and it was off.

None of this was good.

When Garrett went deeper he found Phil hadn't used his credit cards or bank card in four days either. That was a call for concern, enough that Garrett had called the local PD in Vegas to go to Phil's house for a wellness check. He wasn't home. Good news was when the police walked around his property there were no signs of forced entry.

Good news on the surface. But that didn't mean dick until Garrett found him.

"Thank you for remembering I like extra coleslaw," she mumbled into my chest.

"You're welcome, baby."

"And thank you for having Easton buy cherry, cola, and blueberry so I could pick which flavor I wanted."

"Again, you're welcome."

"I want this to be over," she whispered.

Good fuck, I felt that down to my bones.

I knew the feeling of constant fear. The overwhelming desire to crawl out of your own skin to escape your life.

I wished I could promise her it would be over soon, that things would go back to normal. But for people like her and me there was no going back. Normal was no longer what it used to mean. Normal took on a new meaning when the life you were living was taken from you and in its place was this new life you didn't ask for and didn't want.

"I know you do. Garrett should be calling in soon with an update."

I felt her sigh out a breath and snuggle into my chest.

"I don't want to look at pictures. I know it's weak but I just want to close my eyes and pretend."

That wasn't weak. That was real and honest and fuck if I didn't understand that, too.

"So close your eyes."

"You're working."

"I can hold you and read a report."

Then I thought better of my answer and realized she might not be comfortable sitting on my lap at the table. I snatched the file I was reading off the table, set it on her chest, then wrapped my arms around her and stood.

"Whoa," she breathed.

I made my way to the couch, praising Jesus, Mary, and the Universe all of Zane's safe houses had comfortable furniture. I'd spent ten years overseas living off-grid, which meant most of the time I slept on a bedroll on a not-so-clean floor and sat on shit furniture.

When I sat, I adjusted Bridget and grabbed my file.

"Close your eyes and rest, Bridget."

I felt her nod and wiggle closer. I went back to reading Garrett's report.

As always it was thorough, filling in all the missing pieces from this morning's brief.

Kathy Cobbs had paid Mark over fifty thousand dollars at the time of his arrest. The blackmail had only started three months earlier. I hadn't watched the footage yet, but Garrett gave a detailed description of what was on the drone video.

The email exchanges were also in the file and they read as amateur and careless. Mark thought he was too smart to get caught. Kathy thought her position of power and wealth made her untouchable.

Neither one was correct.

What was interesting was Mark hadn't turned on Kathy when he very easily could've tried his hand at a deal by helping solve a missing persons case that had gone cold. It wouldn't have worked; the CIA wanted him buried. With Mark gone, the Sparrow was theirs with no worry it would get in the hands of anyone else.

The CIA was much like any big corporation buying up patents then never putting them to market. The big corporation just wanted the product so no one else could have it. Unlike the corporate giants, the CIA planned to use the Sparrow. They'd just ensure no one else knew about it. Lucky for them, Mark had fucked up.

I flipped back to the first email Mark had sent Kathy

and read it again. There was something in the email that didn't sit right and there was a typo.

Mark was intelligent to the point he was pompous. I'd bet he read and reread his emails numerous times before he sent them. A typo wouldn't do. He'd find it and correct it before he sent it.

My instincts screamed there was something wrong but I couldn't pinpoint what that was.

Easton came into the living room with his phone to his ear.

"Yeah, he's right here."

No sooner did the words come out of his mouth than his gaze dropped to Bridget and he mouthed, "Sorry."

So much for Bridget getting some rest.

Easton stopped by the side of the couch and whispered, "Garrett."

Bridget pressed her cheek into my chest, a silent communication she was still awake.

"Yeah?" I asked when the phone was to my ear.

"Still can't find Phil, but I did find a second bank account."

"Let me guess, it has fifty thousand dollars in it."

"Actually it only has thirty grand, but yes, it has deposits equaling fifty thousand."

There it was.

The something that didn't add up.

"How'd you find it?" he asked.

"I hadn't put it all together," I admitted. "But the emails were off. I was going to ask you to send me some from Mark's company email address to compare."

"Impressive," Garrett muttered and he sounded like he meant that.

After working alone for so long, rarely having anyone to bounce ideas and theories off of, it had taken some time to get used to collaborating with a team again. Easton, Cash, Jonas, Smith, and I had worked independently, sending our data back to Kira and Layla to analyze. It might've taken some adjustment but I couldn't say I didn't like having my team at my disposal and I sure as fuck liked seeing them every day instead of on the rare occasion we could break protocol and get together.

"We're still not any closer to figuring out who attacked Bridget and the bigger question of how they found her."

"One step at a time. I'm running the emails sent to Kathy against emails from Phil's account through comparison software. Just to double check. But with the deposits matching the withdrawals from Kathy's account I think it's a safe bet it was Phil blackmailing Kathy. However, I want to make sure it wasn't a team effort and it was Phil impersonating Mark. I've already started digging through Phil's life. Smith is helping me with that. We'll have more answers soon. But now I'm wondering if Phil got greedy."

"What's that mean?"

"Did he start blackmailing her again?"

Shit.

"Do you think he's impersonating Bridget now?"

"No. I think Kathy's being careful with clean-up seeing as she'd think with Mark in prison she'd be in the clear. If Phil is back at it, she's now wondering who else on the team knows."

That made sense.

"Does she have the resources inside the Marshal service? And speaking of, how'd the meeting go?"

"Johnson canceled at the last minute. And I'm looking for a connection."

"Why'd he cancel?"

"Said he had a lead he needed to follow up on."

I felt my muscles bunch and my stomach knot. Obviously Bridget felt it, too, and lifted her head.

"Lead?"

"That's what he said. Johnson told Zane he was in Vermont and he'd be in touch when he got back."

I knew Bridget could hear Garrett through the phone when her eyes got big and she frowned.

"Troy," I muttered.

"That's what I was thinking. Do you want to call him or should I?"

Reluctantly I told him, "I'll call him but I'm not feeling good about calling a man I don't know in a situation like this. Especially when Johnson could've picked him up."

"If you give me twenty minutes I'll run Johnson and see if I can get his location."

Garrett was talking about using Patheon, the facial recognition software Kira had developed. She'd licensed the program to law enforcement and government agencies. But there were parts of the program that were held back, namely the highly illegal components which utilized footage from personal and business security cameras. If the footage was stored online Patheon could access it. Anything from a door camera in a neighborhood to a gas station in the boonies.

"I'll wait for your go-ahead before I make that call. You got anything else for me?"

"That's all for now."

"Right. Later."

"Later."

I hung up and blew out a breath.

Bridget was still staring at me with a weary gaze.

"Did you hear?" I asked.

"Phil was blackmailing Kathy?"

"Looks that way."

"And he was pretending to be Mark."

Yeah, she'd heard the whole conversation.

"Again, looks like it."

"I can totally see that."

Easton came back into the living room with a KFC container of coleslaw in his hand and plopped down in the recliner across from the couch.

"Why's that?" he asked around a mouthful.

"I know you're not eating the last of my coleslaw."

Easton flashed her a smile and shook his head.

"No. Theo ordered four coleslaws, so there's plenty left for you."

"Plenty by *your* estimation maybe. Some of us were stuck in a tiny town for months with no KFC for hours. I missed my coleslaw."

"Yeah, well, try living without real pizza for ten years," he volleyed.

Pizza had been a topic of conversation between us while we were overseas. All of us missed good old-fashioned cardboard pizza from Dominos. Sure, there was Dominos overseas but it did not taste the same.

"Fine. You win," she grumbled.

"Phil?" he prompted.

"He's nice enough. His work's a little sloppy because he likes to take shortcuts. I also heard him complaining to Mike about child support. Something about his ex taking him back to court to get more money out of him and he was pissed because if his support went up he'd have to sell his camper."

Phil sounded like a dick who needed to adjust his priorities. Obviously I didn't have kids but I couldn't imagine bitching about taking care of them or wanting to keep a camper more than I wanted them fed, clothed, and happy.

"What about Mike and Sarah?" Easton went on.

Bridget settled back on my chest and it struck me then how natural it felt to have her on my lap, cuddled into me while she was talking to Easton. Not only that, but Easton hadn't batted an eye when he saw her there. Not even a raise of his eyebrow in question.

"What about them?"

"Either of them give you any weird vibes? Did they ever act strangely? Anything."

"I'm not the best judge of weird vibes seeing as my boss was conspiring with a warlord and I had no idea. Neither had I caught on to the blackmail scheme going on. But Mike's a little on the quiet side. He was there to work, period. He was fully engrossed in solving the battery issue. It consumed him more than the rest of us. Sarah liked to gab, mostly about her Instagram followers and how when the project was finished she was going to travel and create content for her IG. Some sort of inspirational content using drone footage flying over beautiful landscapes. She also had plans to sell her footage. She said she just wanted to be free and see the world."

I knew nothing about Instagram or social media beyond the serious security risks it posed. So I didn't understand how someone could make a living creating content and honestly I didn't care enough to know.

"Mike ever talk about his wife? What she did?"

"Yeah, she's a photographer. Mostly nature. She sells her images to major publications."

Before Easton could ask any more questions the motion sensor floodlight went on in the backyard.

Both Easton and I got to our feet. I was still holding Bridget.

"What on—"

"Shh." I glanced at Easton, got a chin lift, and swiftly started down the hall.

"What's happening?" Bridget whispered.

"Not sure. Easton's gonna check." When I made it to the master bedroom I went directly to the closet. "There's a safe room in here. I need you to go inside so I can help Easton."

"What?" Bridget turned to stone in my arms.

"Just to be safe. I'm sure it's nothing but I need you in the room so I can—"

"I can't," she rushed out, tightening her hold around my neck.

I finished punching in the code to open the door. The lock clicked and Bridget started trembling.

"Everything's going to be okay."

"I'm claustrophobic. Like really claustrophobic. If you

stick me in there I'll have a panic attack and won't be able to breathe."

Fucking shit.

She didn't sound scared; she sounded fucking terrified.

"I'm gonna set you down." Her arms turned into steel bands around my neck. "You're not going in the room."

At my assurance she loosened her grip and I dropped her to her feet. I rushed around to my holster and pulled out my Sig. I held it out.

"Quick, baby, I need you to pay attention." She nodded and I continued. "You see this lever right here?" I got another nod. "That's the safety. You click that down and the gun is ready to fire. Do not take off the gun safety unless someone opens the closet door. There is a bullet chambered. Once the safety's off all you have to do is aim and pull the trigger. You have twenty rounds in the magazine. You got that?"

"Yes, but—"

"No buts, baby. That door opens, you shoot. You don't wait to see who it is, just pull the trigger. When I come back I will knock five times. Five, Bridget. Not one or three —five. If someone knocks twice and opens the door. Shoot. Got it?"

"Five times," she repeated.

I handed her my Sig, pressed a kiss against her forehead, and ordered, "Don't leave this closet until I get back."

She nodded and I took off.

When I made it to the living room my phone was buzzing on the kitchen table. Likely the call was from the office belatedly telling us someone had breached the perimeter. I nabbed my phone, saw it was Garrett, and took the call.

The phone wasn't to my ear before he launched in, "Easton's around the front. Back of the house is clear. I'm tracking the target now."

Target, not targets. Yet I still asked for clarification. "Just one?"

"Yes."

"How close did he get?"

The cream shades were drawn, so even if someone got close they wouldn't be able to see in. However, that also meant we couldn't see out but we could see the floodlight coming on to light up the backyard brighter than daylight.

"Lights trip at fifty feet. Alarm alerts at forty feet. The alarm didn't trip. He came over the back wall, lights came on, and he hightailed his ass back over. Easton's being cautious checking the front yard. Camera out there didn't pick anything up."

A forty-foot perimeter alarm was the best we could do in a neighborhood. It wasn't ideal but it was something.

"Did you get a good image?"

"Negative. He was wearing a mask."

A mask?

"The man who attacked Bridget didn't bother."

"Nope."

The back door opened and Easton strode through, deep lines creasing his forehead.

"Easton's back, we gotta roll." I told Garrett something he very well knew.

"House in Fairfax is ready."

Sour hit my gut. I didn't want to think it but it had to be said. "No one followed us."

"I know where you're going with this," Garrett started. "I already have a message out to Shep. I'd like to say I'm a hundred percent sure we're secure but a man in a mask hopping the back fence of one of our safe houses says otherwise."

Yep, that was where my mind had gone.

"So with that, are you sure Fairfax is the best place to go?"

"Yes."

Trust.

This was one of the times when I needed to trust my teammate even though my instincts were telling me to pack up Bridget and go on the run.

"That said, I'm sending you there because the property's in the middle of nowhere. Lots of land surrounding the house. If someone shows up there, time will be on our side."

My chest tightened.

A burn I'd never felt before lit and fury took over.

"I'm not purposefully putting Bridget in danger so we can—"

"It's called a calculated risk," Zane came over the line.

Motherfucker.

I didn't have time to go rounds with my boss.

"Calculated or not, I'm not feeling—"

"You want this done for her," Zane cut in. "If you want her safe and at the end of this her staying in Annapolis—or more specifically in your bed—you'll trust your skills, you'll trust Easton's got your back, and you'll trust Garrett. It's that simple."

Trust.

There was that word again.

Easton started down the hall toward the bedrooms. Before my friend got shot I needed to stop him.

"I wouldn't go back there. She's armed with instructions to shoot."

Easton stopped dead and tilted his head.

"You gave her a gun?"

I ignored Easton in favor of getting Zane off the phone.

"We're headed to Fairfax."

"Damn." Zane whistled. "A man who sees logic and doesn't bitch and cry and throw a hissy fit. I like it. Let's hope your brothers follow suit. I've had enough of grown-men temper tantrums."

I didn't have time, yet I still told him, "I wouldn't count on that. Cash is a big baby who doesn't like to follow directions."

With that, I disconnected and went to get Bridget.

11

ONE. TWO. THREE. FOUR. FIVE.

Five knocks.

Then... "Bridget, I'm opening the door, don't shoot."

My heart had been pounding in my chest for what seemed like hours. My palms were sweaty to the point I was worried Theo's gun was going to drop from my hands.

What if Theo wasn't alone?

What if he'd been captured and someone was out there with him making him knock on the door so I wouldn't shoot?

My mind whirled with different possibilities. All of them scarier than the last.

No.

Theo wouldn't knock if someone was out there. He'd just open the door and let me start shooting.

Oh, God.

What if I accidentally shot Theo or Easton?

The door slowly opened and I held my breath. It opened farther and my heart thumped harder. Finally

Theo's big, beautiful body came into view. I dropped the gun and launched myself at him. He rocked back but easily caught me, wrapping his arms around my back and holding me close.

"Everything's fine. You're safe."

"Easton?" I croaked.

"Getting our bags ready to go."

I didn't lift my head out of his neck when I asked, "We're leaving?"

"Yeah, baby, someone was in the backyard." I tensed and Theo kept right on giving it to me straight. "He got over the fence, the light came on, and he fled. Garrett caught it on camera but the guy was wearing a mask."

"So how do you know it's a man?"

"Don't know for sure. But when I say fence I really mean a six-foot wall. A woman would have to be taller than average and strong to get herself over. And if the person was short and strong as fuck, Garrett would've noted the person could be a woman."

That was kind of sexist. I was sure there were plenty of women who could easily hop a six-foot wall but right then facing another move, I didn't have it in me to stand up for the sisterhood and protest.

Theo walked farther into the closet and in a show of his superior strength he squatted to pick up his gun I'd dropped while I was wrapped around his midsection like a deranged monkey. I couldn't find it in me to be embarrassed. After another terrifying incident I needed him close. I needed his heat and the comfort he gave me and I didn't care what that said about me.

I was over being strong.

I was over being stuck in fight or flight.

I was over preparing for a battle that would one day sneak up on me. I didn't know when it was coming, I just knew it was.

Theo came out of his squat, shut the safe room door—a room I was grateful he didn't make me get into because I wasn't lying. I would've had a full-blown panic attack. I'd always hated small spaces. Hated the feel of being closed in. Nothing traumatic had happened to me, I just didn't like it.

"Thank you for not making me go in there," I mumbled.

"I'd never ask you to do something that would cause you harm."

I believed that. But in this case, giving in to what I wanted put him at risk.

"Did you have another gun on you?"

"There are more weapons—"

"I didn't ask that. Did you give me the only gun you had on your person?"

"Yes. But Easton was armed."

I closed my eyes and shoved my face into his neck.

Yes, he'd put himself in harm's way so I wouldn't have a panic attack.

I both loved and hated that.

"From now on I'll make sure I always carry an extra," he told me.

What he was saying without saying it, was there could be a next time.

I loved and hated that, too.

Love that he was straight with me, something he knew I appreciated because I'd told him so back when he was guarding me. There had been so much going on around me that I had no control over, but he'd always told me flat out, no sugarcoating it, what was happening and why. He gave me a sense of security, even if I didn't like what he was telling me. Now was no different. I'd rather know the unfiltered truth than some watered-down version or nothing at all.

"Thank you for always being honest with me."

"I struggle with that," he told me as he walked out of the closet. "I want to protect you and part of that is I want to protect you from being scared and I can't do that if I'm always telling you what's going on."

God.

I didn't love that, I *adored* it.

"The best way to protect me is to arm me with the information so I'm not blindsided. That scares me more—when I don't know an attack is on the horizon I can't mentally prepare."

Theo stopped by the bed and patted my rear end. I rightly took that as he wanted me to unwind myself and get to my feet. When I was steady he slid his hands up my arms and over my shoulders, until he reached the sides of my neck. He gave me a gentle squeeze, all the while holding my gaze.

"I tell you because you need it, but also because I know you're strong and you can hack it."

That was a nice thing to say though I didn't get to tell him that.

"Proud of you, baby," he whispered. "So damn proud."

I didn't know why it happened. Could've been it had been so long since I'd heard someone tell me they were proud of me. It could've been the way Theo was staring into my eyes. It could've been the adrenaline, or it could've been a combination of all three. Or it simply could've been Theo—the man he was, the strength he exuded. Hearing his praise I felt my eyes get wet with gratitude.

His right hand slipped up my neck, over my cheek, and he used his thumb to brush away an errant tear.

"You did great," he finished.

I didn't feel like I did great.

"I was shaking like a leaf," I admitted. "My heart was in my throat, and the longer I was in there the more my mind started to go to crazy places."

"I bet."

That was another thing I loved about Theo—he never tried to placate me or give empty platitudes. He just gave honesty and moved on.

"I'd like to not have to do that again."

"I'd like for you not to have to do that again, too. But if the time comes when you do, you proved you can handle yourself."

I knew I sounded like a broken record, but I was tired of handling myself. I was so damn tired of waiting for the next shoe to drop. And by shoe I meant the next trauma.

"Ready to roll?" Easton asked from the door.

"Yeah," Theo answered for us.

"I want to grab my coleslaw."

Coleslaw.

That was what my life had come to. Sadly, the most important thing in my life was KFC coleslaw. I had nothing else of importance.

"Already done."

"That was sweet of you," I told him.

"What can I say? I'm sweet like that."

"No, he's not," Theo rapped out. "Generally, he's an asshole."

"Theo!"

Obviously, Easton took no offense if his chuckle was to be believed.

And if not that, the easy way he threw his own jab told the tale of brothers bantering.

"That's rich coming from you, pal. The King of Dick."

"Well, I don't like to brag, but..." Theo let that trail off and I pinched my lips to stop myself from smiling.

Theo indeed had something to brag about. So much so, I was seriously disappointed Theo's promises from earlier were being derailed with another move.

"I'll give you that since your lady's in the room. However, I feel the need to note—"

"No, you don't," Theo cut him off, stopping him from saying whatever he was going to note.

Though, I could guess what that was.

After all, men are nothing but overgrown boys who still like to talk about their penis size.

"Are we leaving or are we going to stand around and compare penises?" I asked. "Because if we are, someone better have a ruler. I might've been born in the morning, but not yesterday morning so I won't fall for nine inches in man-speak when really that means four in the Imperial system."

"Nine inches? Jesus Christ, what the fuck are you packin'? I'm gonna start calling you Long John Silver instead of Two," Easton joked.

I couldn't stop myself from snickering and that didn't stop when Theo narrowed his eyes on me.

"Trust me, baby, he needs no encouragement." Theo paused and sliced his eyes to his friend. "You do that, Three, you'll find I can be creative with my nicknames."

"Do your worst," Easton welcomed.

"Singapore," Theo weirdly said.

Silence hit the room.

I glanced around Theo to see Easton smiling broadly.

"If you're talking about Sofia—"

"I'm talking about the coconut water."

Easton's smile grew and he shrugged.

"Who knew coconut water gives you diarrhea? Besides, every now and then it's good to cleanse your colon."

"Right. Maybe when you're alone and not sharing a hotel room with four other people. The sounds you were making were otherworldly. You sounded like a dying rhino mating with a giraffe."

Unperturbed, Easton shrugged again.

"You could've left the room. Yet you stayed to listen. What's that say about you?"

"It says I was worried you were going to be swallowed by your asshole."

Seriously.

"As interesting as Easton's explosive diarrhea is, can we maybe move on to a subject that doesn't include death by shitting? Or perhaps leave before the person comes back and kills me for real this time."

Easton sobered immediately and spat, "No one's going to kill you."

I was taken aback by the force of his statement.

"I was just making a joke."

"Right." Easton relaxed a fraction but there were still deep lines between his brows. "No one's going to touch a single hair on your pretty head and you can mark that a promise."

Well then...

It seemed Easton took his job super-duper, double-extra serious.

"I know you and Theo won't let anything happen to me."

Easton studied me a moment longer and looked like he had more to say. Yet he didn't say it. He didn't say anything when he turned and left the room.

"Did I say something wrong?" I asked Theo.

"No, honey," he said softly. "Easton can be intense. Especially when he cares about something or someone. He jokes around almost as much as Cash does but when it's important he's all business. Plus, he has more sense than Cash so he normally stops Cash before he can take a joke too far or do something crazy."

"And he cares about you," I noted.

Theo gave me a sweet smile.

"Yes, and he knows I care about you. So, he'll go all out to make sure you're safe and at the end of this I get what I want."

My heart rate ticked up tenfold when I asked, "And what is it you want?"

"You," he said. "You safe. You happy. You free to make decisions about your future without danger lingering. You in my house, in my bed, and me being part of that future."

Holy...

Holy smokes.

I sucked in a breath and held it. I was too afraid to breathe, to move, to blink and have the last three seconds be a daydream.

"You do?" I asked on an exhale.

"Yep. I want to prove to you I'm worth taking a chance on."

He wanted to prove *he* was worth taking a chance on?

Him?

Theo?

I was the bad bet, not him.

I was the one who'd gotten involved with something that was so far above my pay grade I'd allowed myself to be bamboozled.

"You have nothing to prove," I told him.

"Wrong. I have everything to prove."

With that, he pressed a kiss to my temple and tagged my hand.

"Let's get going. We have a far drive."

"Awesome," I mumbled, not looking forward to another long drive.

BACK BEFORE MY life turned upside down I didn't mind road trips. Actually, I liked them. I could turn up the radio, or listen to an audiobook, or just sit in the silence and think.

Now, after all the moving around I'd done in the last year I never wanted to move again. If I survived this situation the next house I lived in was going to be my forever home. I didn't care if it was a studio apartment with a mini fridge and nothing but a hot plate to cook on. I was settling then that was it. And all this running for my life had officially ruined road trips. I didn't care that I had a hot chauffeur who looked sexy as hell as he drove. Neither did I care I was being carted around in a luxury SUV with soft, comfortable leather seats and a premium sound system.

Again, if I survived I'd be ordering my groceries from Amazon Fresh and having them delivered to my front door. From then on if I couldn't order it online I didn't need it.

I glanced over at Theo and watched him check all of his mirrors before he switched lanes. I knew Easton was somewhere behind us but Theo was still watching for a tail. That was kinda hot, too, in an I-might-die kind of way. Which made no sense because I didn't want to die and I'd rather Theo not have to watch for a tail.

But if he had to do it luckily he looked hot while he did.

"Are you Mediterranean?" I asked.

Without looking at me he muttered, "Huh?"

"Your dark hair and tan complexion," I noted.

"Spanish and Italian."

I could totally see that.

"So you're fashionably late, enjoy wine, and are a hothead," I teased him about the typical stereotypes.

"You got one out of three right. I'm never late. I prefer beer or vodka, and I'll drink bourbon if the situation calls for it, but never wine. And I learned a long time ago to keep my temper in check so you could say I'm a reformed hothead."

"What's a situation that calls for bourbon?" I inquired.

Theo didn't need to think about his answer. "When there's wisdom that needs to be dispensed. The birth of a child. Commiserating with a brother about a breakup. A toast to the fallen."

I was going to ignore the comment about toasting the fallen. I was worried what Theo's answer would be if I asked him how many of those toasts he'd been part of.

"Is Theo your real name?"

Unlike before, Theo took his time with his response.

"No. It's Aaron."

I blinked, then blinked some more as I attempted to wrap my mind around Theo being an Aaron.

No way.

"Is it really?"

"I hear the skepticism, but I'm not sure why you think I'm lying. My real name's Aaron Cardon."

"You don't look like an Aaron," I blurted out.

The inside of the SUV filled with Theo's laughter. Very loud, very happy laughter. I took a moment to think if I'd ever heard him laugh that way before.

"I don't?" he said through a chuckle.

"Nope. You look like a Theo."

"You can thank Layla for the name; she picked it."

I hadn't met Layla though I'd heard the name enough.

"I will when I meet her. That's if I'm *allowed* to meet her," I quickly tacked on, not wanting to be presumptuous but unable to hide my desire to meet more of Theo's friends.

"As soon as it's safe, you'll meet everyone."

That filled me with excitement and anxiety. I hoped he didn't mean all at once. I loved a good get-together and I was social but I could get easily overwhelmed and when that happened I turned a little awkward and talked too much.

I pushed that out of my mind. I had enough to worry about without adding me making an ass out of myself in front of Theo's friends to the list.

It was Theo's turn to ask a question and he went straight to the uncomfortable and heavy.

"I know you never met your dad, but have you ever looked for him?"

My dad.

That wasn't a sore subject—it was a no-go subject.

"Nope."

"Is there a reason?"

There were six-hundred-million-and-seventy-two reasons why.

"No interest."

"Okay, baby, I can tell you don't want to talk about him so I'll drop it."

My heart filled with gratitude while my stomach knotted with guilt. I'd asked him uncomfortable questions about his brother and he'd been open and honest about his relationship and feelings.

I owed him the same.

"It's just..." I started. "I've never really talked about him. My grandmother rightly despised him but she had too much class to say anything bad about him so she never spoke of him. As in never. My mom loved him and never got over him which made my grandmother hate him more. And when I got older, and I understood the life my mom was missing out on because she was still in love with a man who'd abandoned her, I began to hate him, too. Not because he left me before I was born, but because my mom deserved so much more. She was beautiful and funny and had this huge heart that she shared with everyone she knew. She never met a stranger, as the saying goes. She just loved freely and spread kindness. But there was this hole inside of her and it wouldn't heal."

I paused to breathe through the pain that thinking about my mom caused. The pain of knowing she died loving a man who didn't love her back.

"One time my mom told me to be careful who I gave my heart to. She said that different people would come in and out of my life, that I'd experience crushes and infatuations, but when the real thing happened—that once-in-a-lifetime, all-consuming love that stole my breath—I needed to be sure before I gave away my heart because once it's given it could never be taken back. That was who my dad was to her—her once-in-a-lifetime, all-consuming love. She gave him her heart and he didn't want it. Didn't want me either, seeing as he took off the day after she told him she was pregnant with me and she never saw him or spoke to him again. He was just g-o-n-e, gone."

Perhaps spelling out 'gone' was a little overboard, however I felt it necessary to punctuate the goneness that my father was.

He left before I was born and with that he lost the opportunity to know me.

Ever.

Even if he hadn't broken my mother, I'd still have enough self-respect not to allow a coward into my life.

"The fucked-up part is I still wonder," I admitted. "I don't ever want to meet him but I do wonder who he is and what he did with his life. If he got married and had kids. I don't want to wonder about him, but I do. So, there you have it, that's the story about my father. I know it's not much, but it's all I know of him."

There was a long stretch of silence before Theo said, "It's not fucked-up to wonder. It's natural. What's fucked-up is a man got his woman pregnant and took off on her. Worse, he took off on his kid. I get why you wouldn't want to meet him and I agree with you. He left, there are consequences to him doing so, and part of that is not having the honor of knowing you. And make no mistake, Bridget, it's an honor to know you. He's missing out on someone special. He could be remarried and have ten kids but none of them would be you, none of them could erase the black mark he has on his soul. I'd say I'm sorry you missed out on having a dad, but truthfully, I'm sorry he missed out on all the beauty you bring to the world."

He's missing out on someone special.

He missed out on all the beauty you bring to the world.

I didn't know what to say to that.

So I said nothing while I stared at his profile.

I did this for a long time.

We sat there in silence.

Theo drove.

I let my mind wander to the future.

A beautiful future with Theo by my side.

The next thing I knew I was being lifted out of the car with Theo murmuring softly, "I've got you, baby."

I stayed asleep, trusting I was safe in his arms.

12

THE SMELL OF BURNING BACON PULLED ME FROM A deep sleep but it was the smoke alarm going off that had me jumping out of bed.

An empty bed.

Where the fuck was Bridget and how the fuck had I slept through her getting up?

I went to the door, threw it open, jogged down the short hallway, and stopped dead when Bridget and Easton came into view.

"Fan faster," Easton instructed.

"I'm trying! And if you drop me I swear to all things holy I will castrate you," Bridget said from her place on Easton's shoulders, waving a magazine nowhere near the smoke alarm on the vaulted ceiling.

"You weigh like a buck oh five. I've carried rucksacks that weigh more than you. Just fan, woman."

Bridget stopped fanning long enough to smack Easton on the top of the head with the magazine.

"You're bossy."

"You haven't seen bossy, Birdie."

"Ugh. Don't call me that. I hate that nickname. And trust me, I've seen bossy."

No, she thought she'd seen bossy but she hadn't seen anything yet.

"Is there a reason the two of you are trying to burn down the house?" I cut in.

Bridget's head snapped to the side.

"Morning," she chirped and smiled. "The two of us aren't doing anything. Easton was supposed to be cooking the bacon while I made the eggs but he got distracted by his phone. The eggs are perfectly cooked and fluffy. Hope you like your bacon charred."

I didn't like my bacon charred. But I did like the bright smile she was beaming my way.

"Way to throw a guy under the bus."

"Anytime, friend," she teased and the smoke alarm stopped blaring.

"You can let her down now."

Easton sidestepped until he was facing me. What he didn't do was squat down to let Bridget get off his shoulders.

"You're grumpy in the morning," he noted.

This wasn't entirely true. Most mornings I woke up content—not happy, not excited to see what the day would bring, not raring to get up, looking forward to something special. I just woke up. But that morning after carrying Bridget to bed, sleeping with her cuddled on my chest, looking forward to waking, excited to open my eyes and feel her pressed against me, only to wake up with her not there, I was a little grumpy.

Since Easton was right, I circled back to something Bridget said.

"The distraction on your phone wouldn't happen to have been an email from Garrett, would it?"

"Negative. It was an email from Kira and Cooper with honeymoon pictures. And you're welcome, I emailed her back but didn't mention Bridget."

That was a relief.

I glanced up at Bridget to see her smile had faded and hurt had crept in.

Dammit.

"Can you please get my woman off your shoulders?"

"Damn, brother, all you're missing is an animal-skin skirt, a club, and a bone in your hair and you'd fit our ancestral profile. Would you like to bang your chest to round out the sketch?"

Fuck it.

I wasn't in the mood to joke.

I walked the ten feet it took to get to Easton and lifted my arms.

Bridget fell forward. I caught her, and put her on her feet. It momentarily helped lift my spirits when on the way down her foot caught under Easton's chin and she clipped him.

"Damn, woman," he complained.

"You ruined the bacon so I'm not sorry," she griped. "Burning the bacon should hold a stiffer penalty than a little tap to the chin."

"Tap? You nearly took out a tooth."

Exaggeration much?

"We'll be right back," I told Easton and tagged Bridget's hand.

When we made it to the bedroom, I tugged her inside, shut the door, and had my lips over hers. She opened, my tongue slid in, and she groaned.

Beautiful.

Before the kiss could turn into something I couldn't deliver on, I pulled back.

"Good morning, baby."

"Good morning," she breathed.

"Now that that's out of the way, do me a favor, yeah?"

"What's that?"

That came out breathy, too.

From a kiss.

"Don't leave our bed without me knowing."

Bridget blinked before she said, "But you needed to rest. You drove all day yesterday. Sure, we had a couple hour-long breaks at the first safe house but most of the day you were behind the wheel."

It was my turn to blink at her. When was the last time someone cared if I rested? And when was the last time someone did something for me simply out of consideration for my well-being?

"I slept most of the drive last night," she needlessly reminded me. "Then you carried me into bed." Again, I didn't need the reminder, but obviously she had a point to make so I didn't interrupt her. "You took care of me; I was returning the gesture. But even if you didn't carry me in I still would've let you sleep in. I get to take care of you, too."

I wanted to argue and tell her it was my job to take care

of her, but fuck me, it felt good to have her want to take care of me.

"Okay, I see your point."

I was rewarded with a beautiful smile.

"Are you hungry?" she asked.

I wasn't but I'd eat anything she put in front of me if she smiled at me like that again.

"Yes."

"Good. Anything we need to talk about? I'm afraid to leave Easton in the kitchen too long. He doesn't know how to cook."

"Baby, Easton's an excellent cook."

Bridget's eyes narrowed and her forehead creased.

"You mean he lied to me?"

"Lied would be an overstatement," I defended my brother. "But, yes, he was fucking with you. He can cook."

"Bastard," she mumbled.

I didn't tell her that Easton fucking with her meant he liked her. If he didn't he would've been polite and nothing more. No teasing, no fucking around, nothing but bland courtesy.

"One more thing to talk about before we go back out. Kira." I watched as Bridget blanketed her expression. "I'm happy that Easton didn't tell her what's going on. There's a reason none of us are saying anything to her. If she knew you were in trouble she'd pack her and Cooper's bags and rush home. I'm talking same-day flight. She deserves this time away. She and Coop need it. There's never any downtime. It's one case after the next. I love her like an annoying little sister, we all do. One day I'll tell you the whole story, but her brother's murder was part of why my decision to fake my death was so easy. There was shady shit going on, not for the greater good, but for greed. I didn't personally know her then and I didn't know Finn, her brother. I just knew a good man had died. There were other reasons besides. Zane being framed for reporting bad intel was another reason. Garrett taking off and leaving his GB team because he thought his actions got Finn murdered, that's another. There was a series of events that were all connected. Layla was our team leader. Kira ran all of our intel and gave us our missions. She did this for ten years hiding in the shadows. She had no life. No friends beyond Layla. No verbal communication with me or the guys. I want her to have this time. I want it more than I want her help and she's fantastic at her job. She and Garrett together are dynamite. With her help, we'd have everything we need to get you safe in half the time it's gonna take Garrett. I know it's selfish, but there it is, Bridget. I adore that woman and she's finally found her happy and I want her to just enjoy it."

Throughout my long-winded rambling Bridget stared at me with those beautiful eyes that held sympathy for a woman she didn't know.

"I don't care if she could end this tomorrow for me, I don't want her to come home early."

I felt relief sweep through me.

"Thank you."

"Why are you thanking me?"

"Because if we called her in, she might very well be able to end this for you tomorrow. She wouldn't sleep until she found the man who attacked you. She'd stop at nothing to make you safe."

"So she can do that *after* her honeymoon. In the meantime I have you and Easton to keep me safe and Garrett seems to be pretty on the ball."

That made me smile.

"Yeah, baby, Garrett's pretty on the ball," I repeated her understatement.

"I just thought maybe..."

When she didn't finish I filled the silence.

"You thought wrong. I told you last night you'd meet everyone and you will."

She nodded her understanding then went on to explain, "It's just that with everything going on I have these moments of doubt. Or not doubt, it's more like moments when I'm afraid we'll slip back into the way it was before and I don't want that."

"Before? When I fell in love with a woman who I knew would be taken away from me and there wasn't a damn thing I could do about it? Or before when you were so tempting I had to wait for you to go to sleep so I could take a shower and jack off? Or before when I was counting down the days until my heart was torn from my chest? Yeah, Bridget, I never want to slip back there."

"You love me," she wheezed.

"Fuck yeah. And your mom was right. When you give your heart to that once-in-a-lifetime, all-consuming love there's no taking it back so I knew I was facing a lifetime of pain and resentment."

"I thought you didn't like me." She smiled.

"Again, I thought I was facing a lifetime of pain without you. Makes a man a little grumpy knowing he can't have what he wants."

"I fell in love with you when you sat on the couch with me and listened to me talk about my grandma. And I knew you were listening to every word. I knew you likely didn't give a flip about what I was talking about but you were willing to give me your time and attention and do both in a way that made me feel seen."

When she was done I closed my eyes to memorize the sensation flowing over me.

The emotion was far from peaceful. It was violent as it invaded my chest, expanding my lungs, burning her admission into my soul.

"That and you never treated me like I was helpless."

My eyes snapped open to take her in.

No, Bridget wasn't helpless.

She never had been. She had simply been powerless to make her own decisions.

"I win," I told her.

"What?"

"I win. I fell in love with you the first time you argued with me about getting a Slurpee on the way to your deposition."

"That was the first day I met you."

"I know. That's why I win. You didn't tell me about your grandma until I'd been guarding you for three weeks. I remember the conversation and I did give a *flip*. The reason you felt seen is because you were. I saw you then and I see you now. I see the woman who gave up her life to do the right thing. I see the woman who, through all that, never once gave in to what was happening. You got pissed, you argued, you fought for everything you wanted knowing you weren't going to get it but that didn't stop you."

What I failed to tell her was she'd been stronger than I'd been.

I'd given her up without a fight.

I wouldn't make that mistake again.

"You know what sucks?"

I knew a lot of things that sucked.

But I still asked, "What sucks?"

"Easton being in the other room and me not being able to jump you to show you how excited I am that you love me."

That was damn near on top of the list of things that sucked.

Finding her attacker so we could be home in my bed and I could show her exactly how I felt about her loving me back was high on the list of things that *didn't* suck.

"Yeah, honey, that sucks."

"Can I at least kiss you before we get breakfast?"

"No."

"No?"

"If you kiss me, I'll kiss you back. But it won't be your pretty mouth I'm kissing and I won't stop until you come on my tongue and I have you pinned to the bed with my dick inside of you. As you pointed out, Easton's awake and in the kitchen, meaning he'd hear you screaming for me. So, no, you can't kiss me. But I'll kiss you later in the shower when I know he can't hear you come for me."

Her lips parted and her cheeks blushed pink.

"Now I really, *really* want to kiss you."

Fuck. We needed to get out of the bedroom before I stopped caring about Easton hearing.

"Breakfast, woman."

The pink still tinged her cheeks but her eyes narrowed when she said, "How about you order me around when we're not in bed *only* when you're wearing animal skin, carrying a club, and have a bone in your hair. Wait, no, not even then. I might love your whole caveman, bossy, domination in bed but not so much when you're not playing between my legs."

Damn, she was cute.

"How about when I'm playing with your tits? Do you like it then?"

She nodded as the pink deepened.

"And what about when my cock's in your mouth and I order you to finger yourself? Do you like it then?"

I didn't need her to nod. The rise and fall of her chest along with her breath coming out in short choppy breaths said it all.

I stepped closer and lowered my mouth to her ear, making sure I brushed my lips over her cheek before I whispered, "I hear you, Bridget." She shivered and I continued. "What you need to hear is, I will never disrespect you in any way. Not in bed, not outside of it. Now, with that said, I will never wear animal skin or carry a club. And you'll never find anything in my hair. But you wanna role-play, I'll happily oblige as long as that includes me eating your cunt until you can't breathe and you're making those sexy sounds you make when you're swallowing my dick." That got me another shiver and I knew she was onboard. "Glad you like the idea, Bridget. Now let's go get breakfast."

I'd barely been touching her but suddenly she was leaning into me.

"Wait."

I waited.

"I just want to say..." she fizzled out. I felt her take a deep breath and on an exhale she said, "I love you, Theo."

I told her I wanted to eat her cunt until she couldn't breathe and essentially I wanted to hear her choke on my dick and she tells me she loves me.

Christ.

"I love you, Bridget."

It wasn't until we were in the kitchen plating up the food it hit me—she'd called me Theo. Not that she'd ever called me anything else. And she'd hilariously declared I didn't look like an Aaron. But she'd said, 'I love you, *Theo*.' No one, not even my mother had said those words.

Theo was all hers.

And he always would be.

13

Easton was sitting across from Theo and me at the four-seater dinette table, happily shoveling the eggs I'd cooked into his scheming mouth.

"So, Easton, how are the eggs?" I asked.

"Really good," he said around a mouthful.

"But not great?"

He lifted his eyes from his plate and understandably gave me a weird look.

"I hear you're an excellent cook," I went on.

"Caught me."

Yeah, I'd caught him and he looked completely unrepentant.

"Right. So, tomorrow you cook the eggs and I'll fry the bacon."

"No can do," he mumbled before he scooped up more egg. "Tomorrow I'm making French toast with peanut butter glaze."

I had no idea what peanut butter glaze was, but I was there for it.

"So, what, tomorrow you were just suddenly going to whip up a gourmet breakfast and somehow convince me you learned how to cook overnight by watching YouTube?"

"No, I was going to wow you with my culinary brilliance and beg for your forgiveness for lying to you."

I glanced over at Theo and asked, "I thought you said he wasn't lying; he was just fucking with me."

Theo lamely pointed to his mouth and started chewing very slowly.

"Come on, Birdie, I was just fucking with you. Don't be mad."

I hated that nickname. It had started in junior high with the boys making it into a joke, calling me Birdie then whistling. The mean girl then picked up on the stupid name and used it as a way to make fun of me.

"She told you she doesn't like that nickname." Theo found his voice and he did it with a mouthful of food and didn't try to hide the half-chewed toast.

It was kind of gross. Yet, not.

"She knows I'm just teasin' her," Easton shot back.

"*She* is sitting right here," I rejoined the conversation. "And I don't like the name because it was used to make fun of me when I was in school."

"Kids are dicks," Easton said. "Didn't get it when I was in school, don't get it now. If it really bothers you I won't say it again. But I'm not making fun of you. I think you get we all have nicknames and sometimes those nicknames change daily if someone does something stupid. It's not us being dicks, it's us showing love."

I thought about what Easton said, and since I'd witnessed the banter firsthand, I got it. Friends teased.

They laughed at each other, not to be mean but to show love and friendship. How many times had Brit laughed at something stupid I'd done—a trip on the sidewalk, or when I mispronounced a word, or when I had a typo in a text? Loads of times.

Easton was right, that was what friends did.

And if Easton considered me a friend I welcomed the teasing.

"I don't mind if you call me that."

I felt Theo's gaze and looked over at him. He was studying me carefully then without a word or reason he leaned over and kissed my temple. Thankfully, he'd swallowed his food.

"Need to call Troy this morning. I meant to do it last night."

What Theo left out was he couldn't do it last night because someone had found us and we had to move houses. Which was more than a little concerning and something I was trying my best not to freak out about. I'd been under witness protection for months before the trial. I'd been taken to and from different office buildings for meetings and switched houses after each of those meetings and no one had ever found me.

Why now?

How?

Troy.

I would concentrate on Troy.

"I hope he's okay."

"He strikes me as a man who can take care of himself."

I wanted to sigh, but I didn't. I understood why Theo

sounded so distrusting. But he didn't know Troy the way I did.

"He saved me," I whispered. "I was at that truck stop scared to death. I had no safe options. I needed to get as far away from New York as I could and I needed to do it quickly. I was terrified when I got into his truck that my body was going to be found in a shallow grave on the side of the road and I was going to end up on one of those whodunnit shows. I stopped being scared when Troy asked me if the man who hit me *got his*. What he was really asking was if the man who hurt me got the shit knocked out of him. Then he stopped and got me ice for my black eye."

Theo's eyes darkened and I wondered if I was doing the right thing by telling him all of this. But he was always straight up with me. As he said, I could hack it. For him to understand why I trusted Troy I needed to give it to him straight, not sugarcoat it or leave something out because it was uncomfortable to say or for him to hear.

"Go on," he growled.

"He drove me all the way to Annapolis because he didn't want me hitchhiking. He wouldn't let me stay in the rundown motel I chose because it was cheap and I had limited cash on me. And when I say he wouldn't let me I mean like you wouldn't let me—not in a creepy way. He offered to stay in his truck if I wasn't comfortable with him staying in a room next to me. He just wanted to watch over me. So, I get it. I understand why you're leery and I'm not trying to convince you not to be. I love that you are, because that says you're protecting me. I just want you to understand why I trust him. I was at his mercy. If he was so inclined, he could've hurt me. But instead he went out of his way to make me as comfortable as he could and did everything he could to get me to you. Which he did. He knew I needed to get to you, he knew I believed you were the only person who'd get me safe, so he made that happen."

I had all of Theo's attention. This was one of those times when he made me feel seen. When I knew he was fully engrossed in every word I said. I could tell by the way his eyes went sharp and the way his brow furrowed in concentration.

"I'm glad you understand why I'm leery. I can't say I trust him, but I can say I'm glad he made you feel comfortable. He also has my gratitude for getting you safely to me."

Theo stalled out for a few seconds and I knew that pause. He did it before he was going to give me honesty. I found I was correct when he went on, "But I've seen good men flip. I've seen otherwise decent men be forced to do things they didn't want to do. I'm not saying that's happened with Troy. What I'm saying is there are a handful of people I would trust your life to and Troy is not on that list. I'm going to call him like I promised out of respect for what he did for you. I'm going to assure him you're safe because I know you're grateful to him and want to ease his mind. I also need to know if he was the lead Johnson was talking about and if he was, what he told Johnson."

I nodded. "Please, just be..."

Be what? Gentle? Nice?

"Bridget, I'm gonna be the only way I can be. And I need you to trust I'll take care of you and the situation."

"Of course, I trust you," I quickly told him.

"Good."

I got another temple kiss before he pushed back from the table, taking his plate with him.

"Are you done?"

I glanced up to see he was talking to me.

"Yes, thank you."

Theo grabbed my plate and looked over at Easton with a raised eyebrow.

"Look at you all house-trained." Easton pushed his plate to the middle of the table.

"Says the man who wears an apron when he cooks."

"You wear an apron?" I giggled.

"I am secure in my manhood," Easton said by way of his answer.

"Will you be wearing this apron when you serve me my French toast and peanut butter glaze?"

"Hey, no one said anything about serving."

I heard the water go on in the kitchen. When I turned and looked, Theo was doing the dishes.

I wouldn't dare call him house-trained but it was a huge plus knowing he did dishes.

He said he'd never wear animal skin but he did say he'd be up for role-play. I wondered if I could talk him into a little Maid and Mistress of the house. I could sit on the couch with a glass of wine and watch him vacuum. He'd be shirtless of course. That was, until he got to the mopping—then he'd be naked.

Yes, a naked Theo mopping would be sexy as fuck.

"Earth to Birdie," Easton called.

"Huh?"

"I'm not gonna ask because your red cheeks give you away."

What was he talking about?

"Who has red cheeks?"

Easton smiled. Which wasn't unusual, but I'd never seen his face go soft while he was smiling or any other time.

"You do, Bridget, and they tell me you're into him as much as he's into you. Well, they actually say you were thinking about his Long John Silver but I'm still traumatized to learn my brother's packing some serious heat so we're gonna go with the G-rated version of why you're sitting across from me spacing out with a pretty blush on your face. And all I have to say about that is I'm happy for him."

I appreciated Easton going with the G-rated version.

And I really needed to work on my cheeks turning red.

"Happy for him but not for me?" I teased.

Easton leaned in closer and was not teasing when he said, "Happy for you, too. I know my friend, I know the man he is, I know he'll bust his ass to make you happy. No offense but I'm happier for him. After what he's been through, what he gave up, he deserves a woman like you. He needs a woman who can match his strength. A woman who is strong enough to stand by his side and ease a decade's worth of burden. Yes, I'm happy for you. But I'm pleased as fuck my brother found his one."

I'm not sure how Easton thought I'd find offense that he was happier for Theo when that came with the compliment he thought I was strong and the right woman for the man he called brother.

I didn't tell Easton this but I knew he read me when he tipped his chin and smiled.

"It's about time you called," Troy complained as soon as Theo greeted him.

I glanced from Theo down to Theo's phone on the coffee table. I was on my knees next to the table. Theo was sitting on the couch, leaning forward, resting his forearms on his thighs. Easton was sitting in a chair listening.

I'd promised if Theo put the call on speaker so I could hear the conversation I wouldn't say anything. But with Troy's opening I was having a hard time not reminding Troy to be nice.

"It's only been a few days," Theo reminded him. "I told you I'd be in touch."

Without being asked, Troy confirmed Theo's suspicions. "Got a visit yesterday from a Deputy Johnson and Deputy Caraway."

Theo sat up straight and asked, "What'd they want?"

Troy huffed like he thought Theo was a little dense.

"They asked me if I'd seen a woman named Brenda King. I told them I had no idea who Brenda King was. Which was not a lie; I know three Brendas, none of them with the last name King."

I glanced at Theo and wasn't surprised when he looked impatient. I wouldn't have been shocked if he started using his hand to motion for Troy to hurry his story along.

"Then Deputy Johnson loads up a video on his phone and shows me and Cindy walking into a gas station together and asks again if I'd seen Brenda King. Of course my answer was the same, I don't know a Brenda King."

Oh, shit.

Theo turned his head to look at Easton. My gaze followed and I caught a silent exchange. Not that I knew what Theo was communicating but clearly Easton did because he pulled out his phone.

"How was Johnson behaving?"

"Behaving?"

"Was he aggressive with you? Agitated, impatient, concerned, on edge?"

"Well, the man thought I was lying to him so I'd say impatient but not aggressive."

"What about Caraway?"

"Edgy, if that means looking around like someone was watching us. Very impatient."

I settled on my behind and shifted my legs to the side. I did all of this with my eyes on Theo. Suddenly he was the one who looked edgy and very impatient.

"Was someone watching you?"

"I was being questioned at a truck stop in bumfuck Ohio by two men in suits. Of course we were being watched."

Poor Troy. I hoped he wasn't embarrassed.

"What truck stop?"

"Circle K off 30. Technically it's over the Ohio river about three miles into West Virginia. Chester's the town."

"How'd Johnson take it when you told him the truth?"

"The truth," Troy spat. "The truth is, I met a woman whose husband beat her up and she was running for her life. She told me her name was Cindy. I took her as far as I could and dropped her off in Philly."

I closed my eyes.

He covered for me.

He lied to the US Marshal Service and put himself in jeopardy for me.

"Did they say anything else?"

"Sure, they said lots of stuff about how I could go to jail for hindering an investigation. Blah. Blah. Blah. When I asked why Cindy was being investigated Caraway jumped in quick to tell me they couldn't comment on an ongoing investigation. So I told Caraway I no longer felt like helping with an ongoing investigation and told them the next time they wanted to talk to me they'd have to do it official-like, with a warrant. Johnson didn't seem happy that his young partner was snappy with me. But he thanked me for the information and they left."

They'd threatened Troy with jail and he hadn't flipped.

I never doubted it, but I was right about Troy. He was good and kind and trustworthy.

"I know I asked you to call me and check in," Troy went on. "But I'm seeing now this is more serious than I thought. I won't hold you to your promise as long as you promise me now she's safe. And I find out later you lied to me, I'll shoot you dead. I'm serious about that. I'm an old man but a damn fine shot."

I sucked in a breath, positive Theo was going to go ballistic. But he shocked the hell out of me and smiled.

"You have my promise. And if I fall down on that job I'll stand in front of you and let you put me out of my misery."

"I'm not going to ask you any questions. I've seen those shows so I know those assholes can listen in on phone calls. By the way, I love the IRS and the fine men and women who work there. I'm a hardworking, honest man, and file those taxes on time and truthfully."

Theo's smile widened.

"I hear that. The IRS is great. I'll let you go, thanks for taking my call."

"Hope I get another one."

The line disconnected and I asked, "What in the world was he talking about the IRS for?"

"He was being funny, thinking the government was listening."

Holy shit.

"Can the government do that?"

"They can do whatever the fuck they want to do. But no; if Troy's phone is tapped all they'd hear is static when the call connected. The government might be listening in on Troy's line—though that's doubtful—but they cannot tap my phone. Advantage of having Garrett and Kira."

Yes, Garrett. The one who got Z Corps' information wiped clean.

"When I get a phone again I want one of Garrett's magic phones that telemarketers can't call and the government can't tap."

"I'll hook you up."

"Garrett's already pulling the security feeds," Easton announced. "Zane wants to wait to see if Johnson reaches out for another meeting."

"Bridget?" Theo softly called my name. When I turned

my attention from Easton back to him he continued, "You were right."

"So, you trust him?"

"No, but that's only because it takes a long time to earn my trust, especially when what I'm trusting someone with is special to me. But I do believe he'd put his ass on the line for you."

Well, that was something.

Not to mention, I was the someone special he was talking about so I couldn't be upset Theo still didn't trust Troy. But he did acknowledge Troy was a good guy.

14

I WAS AWAKE AGAIN BEFORE THEO.

But today, I didn't jump out of bed so he could sleep. I also didn't hear Easton get up like I did yesterday morning. Though, last night before I went to bed I heard Easton tell Theo he'd take the night shift again. So I knew he was awake and would be until Theo was awake and he could go to sleep.

I peeked over at the window, didn't see any light coming in through the blinds, and decided it was too early to be awake. Especially with Theo's hard chest pressed tightly against my back, his arm around my middle, his hand resting on my stomach. I scooted back, closing the fraction of an inch that separated us and snuggled into his warmth.

I closed my eyes and went back to sleep.

The next time I woke up I felt Theo's fingers gently stroking my stomach. His firm body was still wrapped tightly around mine with the addition of a very thick, very long erection resting on my panty-covered ass.

"*Mmm,*" I hummed and pushed my ass deeper into his crotch.

"Morning, baby," he returned, gliding his hand up under the shirt I'd worn to bed.

When he reached my breast he cupped it, brushed his thumb over my nipple, then added his finger and rolled the tightened bud with just enough pressure that I arched into his hand wanting more.

"Panties off," he bossed. "Unless you don't mind losing another pair."

I absolutely, one thousand percent did not mind losing another pair if that meant I got to experience the pleasure of him tearing them off of me. Unfortunately, my undie selection was currently limited, so practicality won out over having the mini orgasm I knew watching his strong fingers tear through the lace would cause.

I shimmied out of my panties, got them to my ankles, and kicked them off.

"Open yourself up for me, Bridget," he ordered. "Leg over my thigh."

God, his rough, scratchy, morning voice was sexy as hell.

I did what he asked, taking the sheet with me, exposing myself to the cool air of the room. It felt good against my heated skin. Throughout this, Theo kept rolling and pinching my nipple. Not hard, not gently, somewhere in the middle.

I wiggled back, wanting more.

Theo was having none of that.

"Stay still."

I didn't want to stay still, I wanted him to hurry. I

wanted all the things he'd promised but circumstances yesterday were such he couldn't make good on those promises. That didn't mean I hadn't thought about it all day —hoping he'd get a break from work to give me a little relief. And I knew he'd thought about it, too. More than once I'd caught him staring at me, eyes heated, jaw tight.

I was ready.

More than ready.

And before the next disaster hit, I was going to get it.

So, I disobeyed him and ground my bare ass against his erection.

His welcomed response was to pinch my nipple to the point of pain. Delicious pain that brought with it a flood of desire.

"Is that what you wanted?" he asked as he continued to abuse my nipple.

"Yes," I groaned.

I wanted to groan for a different reason when he let go of my nipple and slid his hand back down to my stomach, giving me nothing more than his fingertip gently trailing from hip to hip.

"Theo," I snapped.

"Good girls get good things," he rasped against the side of my neck. "You want good things, Bridget?"

I nodded.

"You gonna be a good girl?" he asked.

I wanted to say yes. I wanted *all* the good things Theo could give me. But saying yes would be a lie. I was too impatient to be good. The evidence of that impatience had gathered between my legs.

I shook my head no.

"Didn't think so."

His hand drifted lower to my thigh and he hitched my leg higher. Whisper-soft, he skated his fingers down the inside of my legs, over my wet center, up to my clit before he skimmed back down.

Slowly.

Up and down he went.

Giving me nothing but want.

Building the ache until I was ready to explode.

"You gonna be good now?"

I thought I was being stupendous, controlling my need to roll him to his back and slam myself down on his cock.

I shook my head no.

Without warning two fingers slammed inside of me, pulling a startled gasp from my throat.

"How about now, Bridget, you gonna be good for me?" His fingers pumped in and out roughly. "Move with me. Fuck yourself on my fingers."

I moved the best I could while being captured between the hard wall of muscle at my back and his hand working between my legs. But in no way was I fucking myself—Theo was doing the finger fucking and he was doing a spectacular job of it.

I squirmed back, hoping he'd understand I was ready for more.

"You want my cock?" he growled and ground his erection against my ass.

"Yes."

I felt him shift away from me, twist, move, then he was back, his bare dick now sliding between my legs. I missed his fingers but this was better. The head of his dick nudged my clit and I jolted.

"So fucking wet," he groaned.

Drenched was more like it.

"And ready," I added.

"Told you before but it bears a repeat, this changes everything. I won't let you go. Be very sure this is what you want."

"This changes nothing," I told him and tipped my head back in offering. "I was never going to let you let me go. I was prepared to beg you not to let me leave."

Theo went solid behind me. The only movement in the bed was the vibration coming from his chest as he rumbled out a tortured moan.

His hips pulled back then he slammed into me.

Full.

So full I cried out.

Electricity shot down my spine, the charge so forceful I arched into it and thrust back.

"This is your punishment," he grunted.

His hand joined his cock between my legs, his fingers danced over my clit, and for a second I was worried he was going to tease me until I broke.

I quickly found I was wrong.

Theo was intent on breaking me a different way.

And that was by building my orgasm so fast I couldn't catch my breath. His fingers on my clit rubbed, circled, and pinched—all with an expertise that shocked me. Like he knew exactly how to touch me to get maximum results. Though I wasn't sure I needed that extra stimulation, I could come by his cock alone. He pounded deep and rough, stretching me, hitting places I didn't know existed, grinding and gliding in and out until I was mindless.

I could think of nothing else except his cock, my pussy, and the overwhelming need to climax. Those thoughts were fleeting seeing as I was already there. So close to the edge I was powerless to slow it down. I didn't tell him I was there. I didn't say a word or utter a sound mainly because I couldn't breathe.

My body jerked with the first wave of pleasure. I tensed as it consumed me, my toes curled, and my pussy convulsed.

I broke.

And I broke some more.

Oh, yeah, I broke with the most intense orgasm of my life.

"Jesus fuck," Theo groaned.

If I had any wits about me I would've echoed his musing.

Jesus fuck was right.

I was still in a haze of euphoria when he pulled out, rolled me to my back, hooked my leg over his arm, and drove back in.

"Look at me, baby."

I righted my head, brushed my hair out of my face, and stared up at his beautiful face.

"Can you take more?"

I could take anything Theo was willing to give me.

I nodded.

"Hands above your head, brace your palms on the headboard."

I brought both my hands above my head and braced myself.

His gaze dropped to my chest.

He fell to one elbow and used his other hand to pull my shirt up to my neck.

"Beautiful," he mumbled as he lowered his head, taking a nipple into his mouth and sucking hard.

He released it and moved to the other side, this time slowly circling it with his tongue until it peaked.

I couldn't stop myself from squirming.

His eyes tipped up and narrowed.

"If you want me to stay still then you're out of luck," I told him and bucked my hips. "It's impossible when your big dick is planted deep and your talented mouth is playing with my nipples. And if that was your idea of punishment, let's just say I plan on being bad. Very, very bad."

Theo's lips curved up arrogantly.

He knew he broke me and he knew I'd enjoyed every second of it.

Further from that, he was counting on me not being able to stay still so he'd have an excuse to "punish" me.

He kissed my nipple before he came back up over me, slowly withdrawing his hips before deliberately sliding back in, giving me gentle after he'd fucked me hard.

"This is for me," he whispered. "I want those pretty eyes on me the whole time. I want to watch it build before I tear it down. Can you do that for me?"

"Yes."

I waited for it and smiled when I got it.

"Being a good girl for me."

I totally was.

"Right. Now wrap your legs around me."

I locked my ankles at the small of his back and it was a good thing I did because his next drive wasn't gentle. Neither was the one after that or the one after *that*, and once again my world narrowed—this time to the two of us with my eyes locked onto his while he fucked me hard and deep but not rough. His thrusts were measured, precise, controlled.

I loved every second of this. So much so I lost myself and moved my hand off the headboard.

Theo planted deep, ground his pelvis against my clit, and drew a groan out of me.

"You want my cock, you'll do as I ask."

Except Theo didn't ask.

He demanded.

But I caught his point and put my hand back where he wanted it.

He lowered his face to my neck and nuzzled me there so sweetly I broke another rule and closed my eyes.

"Love you, Bridget," he whispered in my neck.

I would swear my heart swelled five times in size and threatened to burst.

I opened my eyes when he lifted and resumed his relentless pace. His drives were so powerful my head would've banged against the headboard if I wasn't bracing myself. Theo's gaze roamed my face and there again I felt seen in the most beautiful of ways.

I had his attention because he was fucking me. But I had all of his attention because he was fucking *me*.

Me.

The woman he loved.

He was fucking me yet he wasn't. Not in the traditional use of the word. With each glide of his dick I felt the truth of his affection.

"I love you," I panted.

"Theo," he grunted. "I love you, Theo."

"I love you, Theo," I mimicked and watched his eyes flare.

I didn't know the why behind that flare and I didn't care why it meant something to him when I added his name. I just cared that it did and made a mental note to say it again.

A few minutes later I found I was right; I didn't need his finger working my clit. I could come with his dick alone.

"Theo," I gasped.

"Feel it, baby."

I bet he could, what with the power my orgasm had when it snuck up on me.

My hips lifted of their own accord, chasing the orgasm that lingered just out of reach.

It was then I learned the true meaning of Theo's dominance. I learned what he meant when he said good girls get good things with blinding clarity.

He demanded, bossed, and took.

I followed his orders and reaped the rewards.

"Jack your knees up higher, baby, I want deeper in your pussy."

I jacked my knees higher.

Theo slid deeper, my womb contracted, and I moaned.

"Can you breathe?" he asked.

I could, barely, but enough to answer, "Yeah, honey."

Theo smiled down at me, his eyes full of lust and desire and something else.

Mischievous if I had to guess.

"That won't do. I want you breathless when you come around my cock." To punctuate his meaning his thrusts turned savage.

He indeed stole my breath and my mind and my soul as my body ignited into nothingness.

Nothing but pleasure. Every nerve tingled. Every muscle bunched. My limbs trembled.

"Fucking beautiful," he grunted. "Come for me."

I also learned my body obeyed him without question.

"Fuck," he rasped. "Fucking hell, your pussy is so goddamn beautiful."

As compliments went, it wasn't flowery but it was Theo. And like everything else, I'd take anything he wanted to give me.

He slowed his pace and took me through my climax that was no less intense but much longer than the first. When I felt myself come back from the blissful journey I had taken, Theo pulled out, shifted to his knees, and palmed his hard dick.

"Watch me," he demanded.

My gaze stayed glued to his hand jacking his dick in long, fast strokes.

"This is yours," he groaned. "This, baby, is what you do to me."

With that he anointed my stomach with thick jets of come.

"Fuck," he grunted and bucked his hips into his stroking hand.

The last thirty minutes had been the most erotic of my life. But I would trade the two orgasms I had—and that was saying something since they were otherworldly—just to watch Theo come on my stomach again.

With one last violent stroke he squeezed just under the head of his dick and his big body shuddered.

"Christ," he bit out.

I lifted my eyes to find him watching me carefully.

"Hands down, that was the sexiest thing I've ever seen," I told him.

Something that looked an awful lot like relief passed over his face.

Did he really think I wouldn't have enjoyed that?

"As sexy as that was," I started with a smile. "You wasted it."

Theo returned my smile.

"Sorry, baby, that was selfish."

"It was. But as noted it was sexy so I'll let it slide this once if you promise next time you aim a little higher so I can taste you."

"Fuck, you're perfect."

"Why, because I swallow?" I rolled my eyes and tacked on, "Such a man."

"*Your* man," he corrected. "And no, you're perfect because you take me as I am, let go, enjoy the fuck out of what I'm doing, and get off on it."

Well, that was an understatement but I let it go without correction.

Instead I focused on the first part of what he said.

"My man."

I knew it came out breathy when his face got soft.

"Yeah, Bridget, yours."

Holy shit on a shingle, I *loved* that.

"Can I ask you something?" I asked.

Theo's eyes went to my belly and he asked his own question. "Do you need to ask me this while my come's drying on your stomach or can I clean you up first?"

That reminded me...

Theo was on his knees naked between my legs. And what I was reminded of was that I had the perfect view of his body. So I took my fill and allowed my eyes to roam all over his muscled chest, the ridges and valleys of his stomach, the happy trail of hair that started as a dusting under his bellybutton but got thicker the closer it got to his cock. I loved that he didn't do what I'd heard a lot of men did now—manscaping—or if he did, he didn't go overboard. He looked masculine and natural. Cut hips, his heavy dick now soft as it rested against his thick thigh.

He was perfection.

All of him.

And mine.

Finally my gaze went to his come drying on my stomach.

"I take it you liked me marking you."

"No, I loved it," I returned.

"What's your question?"

Right, my question. Something that had sprung into my head last night and I meant to ask then, but I was so tired I fell asleep before Theo was done brushing his teeth.

"Back before, when you were guarding me, did you arrange to be the one guarding me during the day?"

"Not at first. But after the first week, yes, I made it so I was the one there while you were awake."

I loved that.

"And dinner?"

"Yes, I pulled a double shift so I'd be there from when you woke up until you were ready for bed. Normally, there'd be three rotations. But I wanted your time and that included eating dinner with you every night."

My smile came so quick it was a wonder I didn't strain something.

"I see you like that."

"No, I love it," I echoed my previous correction.

"Right."

There was a loud knock on the door followed by, "Yo! If you two love birds are done in there, the peanut butter glaze isn't gonna stay soft forever. Chop, chop, get the lead out."

I pinched my lips to stop myself from laughing.

Theo didn't pinch his lips and didn't look like he wanted to laugh.

"Get the fuck away from the door!" Theo shouted.

"Put your Long John Silver away and get the fuck out here. I want to eat and get some sleep."

"Christ."

I lost the battle and busted out laughing.

Best morning ever.

15

"She what?" Bridget fumed and set her fork down.

I just finished updating her on Mike and Sarah.

Cash made it to Maine, got to Mike and his wife, explained the situation sans the attack on Bridget seeing as she was "dead", and they readily took him up on Zane's offer to send them on vacation to a secure location until the situation was under control.

Sarah, not so much.

Garrett sent a man he knew from San Diego to Utah to talk to Sarah. She didn't feel like taking an all-expenses trip courtesy of Zane Lewis. Apparently she was in the middle of getting footage of some conservation area outside of St. George and was on a deadline for some studio. It had taken some convincing to get her to go back to California. And by convincing I mean a two-hour argument.

"She was not happy," I repeated.

"She's normally really sweet and easygoing," Bridget reported.

That was not what the man on the ground relayed. He told Garrett she was a pain in the ass.

"But she's safe?"

"She was headed to California last night, so yeah."

"As fascinating as all this work talk is, can we please discuss the deliciousness that is my peanut butter glaze and the perfection of my French toast?" Easton barged into the conversation, setting down his third helping.

"Jesus, I don't know how you can eat all of that."

"Not all of us are blessed with a nine-inch Johnson, brother, but there are those of us who were blessed with a superior metabolism."

My cock wasn't quite nine inches but it was close enough that I wasn't going to squabble over a few hash marks on a ruler.

"Can we not talk about my cock at the breakfast table in front of Bridget?"

Easton made a show of jerking back in his chair, his gaze ping-ponging between me and Bridget.

"First, if someone wanted to talk about my big dick in front of my woman I'd be all for the ego stroke. Second, I presume at this juncture your woman knows the size of your cock, and if she doesn't she now knows she has something to look forward to."

Bridget knew exactly what she had to look forward to and it was more than just my big dick. Not that I'd discuss my sex life.

"We'll test that theory when you bring your woman to breakfast," I told him.

"You have a woman?" Bridget asked. "Do I get to meet her?"

"No, I don't have a woman and that right there is one of the reasons why. Women flock together and when they do they form friendships. Friendships mean you take each other's back. So, say things don't work out between me and this woman, I can't just scrape her off and quietly move on because she's now friends with my friends' women. It becomes complicated and messy. I don't like complicated and I don't do messy."

"So doesn't that mean you're never going to find a woman and settle down?" Bridget pushed.

"What that means is I'm enjoying being me, doing what I want, going where I want, on my time for the first time in ten years."

I got what Easton was saying. Ten years was a long time to live in the shadows. Move from place-to-place unseen. Living in shitholes, eating shit food, having to be where you're needed when you're needed with barely any down time.

But I disagreed with him on one point.

The right woman didn't complicate your life—she enriched it. The right woman allowed you to be you. As far as doing what I wanted, when I wanted, on my time, I'd rather share that time with Bridget.

"That's alright, Easton," Bridget said. "I have a long memory and one day you'll cave and find a woman to bring to breakfast. When you do, she and I will have a lengthy discussion about penis sizes and compare notes." Bridget paused and smiled. "Hope you measure up, bud, because women don't care about metabolism on a man; they care about girth. Size matters."

Easton groaned.

"So what I have a tiny dick but I can cook."

"I don't believe you have a tiny dick."

Christ, was this really happening?

"You don't? Wanna check for—"

"And with that you're done, asshole." I glanced over at Bridget and informed her, "Baby, he's fucking with you. That's one of his lame pick-up lines."

She scrunched her nose and asked, "Does that actually work?"

"Shockingly well. I can't tell you how many times he's taken a woman to the bathroom to prove he has a tiny dick." I looked back at Easton. "Fuck you for making me explain to her that you con women into showin' them your dick."

"I don't con women." He feigned offense. "Tiny is a relative term. What constitutes tiny to one man is a solid twelve inches to another."

"There's no way—"

"Baby," I groaned. "He's still fucking with you and you keep falling for it."

"Theo's right, you're an asshole." Bridget stood and picked up her plate. "You're lucky your French toast is the best I've ever had or I'd end our friendship."

"Best you've ever had?"

Bridget smiled sweetly at Easton, balanced her plate in her left hand, brought the right one up, and flipped Easton off before she turned and went into the kitchen.

"I think I'm in love," Easton said and shoveled a huge bite of French toast into his mouth.

"I know I am," I returned. "So you think you can tone down—"

"Wait," he interrupted me. "You know you're in love with her?"

Was he dense?

"Fuck yeah."

He set down his fork, picked up his mug, and studied me over the rim.

"And that's it?"

"Not tracking?"

"You're ready to settle down? I mean, settle all the way down. You don't want to date her awhile? Hang out? Take a few years to make sure she doesn't have a personality transplant and turn into a raving, crazy person?"

I didn't know who fucked Easton over but I knew someone had. This was not the first time he'd talked about a woman turning into a raving, crazy person.

"Life's taught me a lot of lessons. One of the most valuable is not to waste time."

"Life's short," he mumbled.

"It's fleeting. Temporary. If I know I only have an unknown number of years and I've already lived forty-one of them why in the fuck would I waste days, weeks, months, *years* when what I want is right in front of me?"

Easton took a sip of his coffee then shared, "I'm happy for you."

"I'm sure you are but you're also worried. And I have to say, I love you for that. I know you're looking out for me. Being a good brother. But while you're doing that, you need to let go of the past and whoever fucked you over."

Easton clenched his jaw.

When the silence turned into Easton's obvious indicator that the conversation was over, I pushed back from the table.

"Great breakfast. Thank you."

By the time I finished helping Bridget with the dishes Easton had left his uneaten food on the table and went to bed.

Fuck.

"THAT RAT BASTARD MOTHERFUCKER," Bridget seethed.

One mystery was now solved but I couldn't call it into Garrett until I calmed a furious Bridget down.

"Baby—"

"No. That lying, conniving, underhanded motherfucker. Wait, I forgot to add, thief. Phil is a fucking thief!" she shouted.

"Jesus, what the hell's going on out here?" Easton grumbled, still half asleep.

Bridget surged up from the couch and whirled on Easton.

"I'll tell you what the hell's going on out here. I watched the video. You know, the blackmail video. And that rat bastard, lying, conniving, underhanded, thieving motherfucker stole *my* personal bird and flew it. Not only that, but he used the footage from *my* drone to blackmail that woman. Do you know what that means?"

Oh, yeah, Bridget was off-the-charts pissed. I decided to lean back in my chair and wait for her to burn out.

Easton ran a hand through his hair and stopped near the couch.

"No idea but I'm sure you're going to tell me."

"Damn right, I'm going to tell you. My name's on the footage."

"Say again?"

"My name, Easton. My. Name. Not only is it in the metadata since he used my personal drone that is registered to me but also I have the time stamp programmed so when you watch the replay in the right-hand corner it says, Bridget Keller. Under that it has the coordinates. Under that it has the date and time. My fucking name, Easton."

"Fuck."

"Fuck's right," she griped. "A thousand fucks is more like it."

In all the time I'd known Bridget I'd never heard her curse so much. Nor had I seen her this irate. I'd seen her pissed, irritated, frustrated near tears, but not outright, off-the-chain furious.

I hated to admit it but it was cute as fuck. Not that I'd ever tell her and I was positive if there came a time when she was furious with me I wouldn't find her turning her ire my way cute. But right then—red-faced, shouting obscenities she was fucking adorable.

"So that's why they're looking for you. They think you're part of the scheme," Easton surmised.

"Or maybe since Mark's in jail and they've started to get blackmailed again Phil's impersonating *me* this time, and since *my* name is on the footage that would easily be believed."

"Fucking hell."

I hadn't thought of that.

I yanked out my phone to report in when the perimeter alarm beeped.

"What's that?" Bridget asked.

I got to my feet, pulled my Sig out of my holster, and started in Bridget's direction as Easton turned and ran down the hall to his room.

"Do you remember how to flip off the safety?"

"Yes."

"Good. Get in the closet. Five knocks, Bridget, or you unload the magazine."

"Theo—"

"Take a breath and get in the closet. Everything's going to be okay."

She nodded but didn't move.

"You have a gun this time, right?"

Fucking hell. I needed her in the closet.

"Yeah, baby, I have a gun."

Easton came back in the room fully dressed with his boots already on.

"Three hundred yards out. Four armed."

Bridget sucked in a breath and froze.

I seriously fucking wished Easton would've waited for a brief moment until I got Bridget in the closet.

"Closet. Now."

"Please be careful."

I fought back the urge to shout.

"We will. Closet."

She turned and ran. I had to trust she'd get herself safely to the closet.

I turned to Easton. "I need you to promise me you'll get Bridget out if this goes bad."

"Promise," Easton grunted. "I'll take the front, you come around from the back. I called Garrett. He only sees the four and the morons are all together."

Thank fuck for small favors.

Easton headed to the front. I went to the side door, locked it behind me, and used my phone to set the alarm.

Not that it would do much good but it would alert Bridget if a door or window had been breached and Garrett would know.

I popped an earbud in and called Garrett.

"Easton's in place," he told me. "I'm connecting the calls."

While I waited for Garrett I pulled my Glock from my ankle holster and moved around to the corner of the house opposite from Easton. He was off to the side in front of me, advancing at a fast clip.

"I have a clear sight picture," Garrett came back on the line. "There's only four. They parked at the road and walked up the drive."

"We're positive they're not local authorities?"

"Nothing indicated that's the case."

Unfortunately that was the best we could do. It wasn't like we were going to walk up to four armed men and ask why they were trespassing.

"Three, headed to the west toward the outcropping. I'm going straight in to draw their attention."

"Copy."

"You sure that's the best course of action, Two?" Garrett asked. "You could stay covered and pick them off."

We could, but I liked to be engaged before I took my shot. It made it easier to sleep at night.

"I'd consider that if I was worried one of them could hit me from two hundred yards."

I peeked around a thick wall of shrubs and got my first look at the four men. Jeans, tees, boots, handguns. No masks. No hats. No glasses. Nothing to try to conceal their identities.

What the fuck?

"Where the fuck did these idiots come from, rent-a-mercenary-dot-com? Did you get facial rec yet?"

"Working on it but so far nothing."

How was it possible nothing had come up? If any of the four had a driver's license Garrett would have a name.

"Please tell me they're not Agency assholes," I groaned.

"Wish I could."

I stepped out from behind the bushes and casually walked in the direction of an old outbuilding. If need be I could be behind it in under five seconds.

When the first shot rent the air I took off running.

Agency or not, I was free to engage.

"Three, take any shot available to you."

As soon as I gave my order I heard the distinct sound of Easton's .45.

"One down."

When I made it to the building I stopped at the corner, pivoted, and reengaged the group. Two men were running in my direction. Both had their pistols raised, wildly shooting, doing nothing but wasting ammo.

Easy day.

I aimed at the man on the right, slowly pressed the trigger, fired, and moved to the man on the left. I waited for him to stop to check on his downed friend. Since he didn't, I repeated the process and on an exhale I fired.

Two shots.

Two down.

Clean.

"Check in, Three."

One final gunshot rang out before I heard, "Two down."

"We're clear," I announced.

"Pack up and head out."

With that, Garrett disconnected.

I jogged back to the house, hopped the steps up to the front porch, and punched in the code to open the door. By the time the lock clicked, Easton was behind me.

"We're headed to a hotel and not calling in our location," Easton ordered.

Perfect.

"My thoughts exactly. I'll get Bridget."

Easton hit the hall first and dipped into his room. I went to the room I shared with Bridget and stopped dead.

My heart jumped into my throat and bile rose fast.

"Baby," I panted as I took in the scene before me.

There was a heap of a ghillie suit on the floor, blood pooling around it, and Bridget standing with her back to the open closet door with the gun pointed at the very dead intruder.

"I unloaded the magazine," she told me. "I waited. There was no knock. I unloaded the magazine."

Fuck.

"Good, Bridget. You did good," I told her and slowly made my way to her.

As soon as I had my hand over hers she loosened her grip on the gun. I twisted our hands, pulled the gun free, and shoved it into the holster at my back.

I scooped her up and without delay she shoved her face into my neck.

"I unloaded the magazine," she repeated.

"You did good."

"What the fuck happened?" Easton roared.

Bridget jolted in my arms and fixed herself closer.

"Call Garrett and tell him we have five bodies, not fucking four, and I want to know why the fuck the alarm didn't sound."

"Copy that."

Easton turned and jogged out of the room.

I nabbed Bridget's backpack—that one day soon I was going to burn—and my bag.

Goddamn fuck.

"It's all good, baby. You did good. I'm proud of you."

She nodded but said nothing.

What a clusterfuck.

16

I WAS LOSING IT.

Whatever hold I'd had on my sanity had splintered.

Ten bullets.

I'd counted each one.

"Stay with me, baby."

I glanced over at Theo.

He was pacing the small hotel room, phone up to his ear, talking to someone—Zane maybe. There had been a lot of growling and menacing rumbling. He sounded positively rabid.

But that wasn't what had me on the verge of a breakdown. And if I was being honest it wasn't even the ten bullets I put into the man who'd opened the closet.

It was because I'd had enough.

When was this going to end?

How long was I supposed to live like this?

How many more times would Theo and Easton put themselves in harm's way for me before something bad happened to them?

"How in the fuck does someone take out the fucking power grid?" Theo raged.

I looked at Easton.

He looked as tired as I felt. He had one hand gripping the back of his neck, his other in the front pocket of his jeans, and he was scowling at Theo.

"I'll look and call you back."

Theo pocketed his phone and prowled to the bed next to the one I was sitting on—the one with all the bags on it.

I watched him unzip his bag and dump it on the bed.

"What are you doing?" I asked.

"Zane says he's positive there's no security breach. I'm positive no one followed us to the last two safe houses. Yet both places have been compromised."

I thought I understood.

"You're looking for a tracking device?"

"Yeah."

I pushed up from the bed I was sitting on and went to my bag.

"You should—"

"You've never treated me like I'm anything but strong, Theo, don't you dare start now. I need to do something to keep my mind busy. I can help you."

I watched as Theo ground his molars and flexed his jaw muscles.

But he made no further suggestions about what I should do.

I opened my backpack and dumped it on the bed.

As soon as I did, Theo straightened and stared down at the contents.

"Shit," he grumbled and reached for the key fob of my old, abandoned car.

"What?"

He didn't answer me. Instead, he pulled his knife out of his pocket and popped open the plastic case. As soon as it was opened he closely inspected the thing for what felt like an eternity.

His eyes closed and his head lolled forward.

"Find it?" Easton asked.

"Yes."

"What'd you find?"

Theo held out the device and in the softest, gentlest voice I'd heard him use he broke the devastating news, "Location tracker in your key fob, baby."

I took a step back and looked down at the offending plastic.

"What?"

"It's okay. Now we know."

"It's my fault?"

Two equally forceful nos filled the room. One from Theo, the other from Easton.

"I should've checked before we left the office," Theo said in an attempt to absolve me of my stupidity.

How dumb was I?

"I tried to do everything right! I dumped my phone, my car, I only took cash with me. I never thought about the stupid key."

"It's not your fault," Easton put in.

"Really, it's not? Then whose fault is it? I'm the dumbass who had the tracking device in my bag leading the bad guys straight to us this whole time."

Theo advanced quickly. His hands came up to cup my jaw, the pads of his fingers pressed in, and he tilted my head back.

"Don't you ever call yourself a dumbass again." Anger was still radiating out of him. His big palms shook. His eyes narrowed. "Not ever, Bridget. You are far from stupid. You did everything right. Do you hear me? Every damn thing. We found the tracker, problem solved, now we move on."

"We move on?"

"Yes. That's how this works. There's always a snag, shit always goes sideways. We fix it and move on."

"I killed someone today!"

Theo lowered his face so he was all I could see. Then in a low, ominous tone he schooled me. "No, Bridget, you didn't kill anyone. You saved your life."

"A man's dead," I argued.

"But you're not."

I clamped my mouth closed because there was no debating that.

"Let's change it up," he rapped out. "You didn't pull the trigger, he killed you. Now you're dead. I dedicate every waking moment to hunting down the motherfucker so I can put a bullet in his head. Now you're dead and he's dead. Either way the moment he decided to enter that house he was a dead man."

"You would've hunted—"

"Yes," he cut me off.

"And put a bullet in his head?"

"No, baby, I would've taken my time and carved out his organs before I allowed him the luxury of death. I was being gentle with the bullet thing."

He was serious. Theo would've avenged my death.

In some sick, twisted way I'd never felt more loved in my life.

"You ready to move out?"

I groaned like a toddler gearing up for a temper tantrum, which wasn't far off from what I wanted to do.

"One more question. Am I going to go to jail?"

"No. That man broke into a house. He was armed and you defended yourself. But it won't come to that because the bodies have been cleaned up."

I decided I didn't want to know what that meant so I stopped asking questions.

"Okay, I'm ready now."

Theo stepped out of my space but didn't go far.

"I'm staying here. Cash is on his way. Zane's already prepped the holding room for you."

"Thanks, Three."

"Why are you staying behind?"

Easton dangled the key fob that Theo had tossed onto the bed.

He was going to use himself as bait to see who came next.

"No! I don't like that plan. Leave the damn thing on the bed and come with us."

"Not my first rodeo, Birdie. I'll be fine."

"Easton—"

"Go with Theo and get yourself safe. This will all be over soon."

"And when it's over will you be alive?" I snapped.

This was not right.

The smile Easton gave me scared the hell out of me.

He faked jovial when he winked and said, "I can't miss my brother walking down the aisle."

I knew he was talking about Theo, and my heart should've thumped at the insinuation that Easton thought Theo and I were getting married.

Obviously, there was no talking Easton out of his plan.

"I want it on record that I am fully, super-extra against this plan. I think all three of us should leave together and you should call Cash and tell him not to come."

"Noted."

I wanted to smack some sense into the hardheaded man but I knew that wouldn't do me any good.

"If something happens to Easton will you dedicate every waking moment to avenging him as well?" I asked Theo.

"Yep."

"Good."

Theo leaned down and kissed my temple.

"Let's pack up and hit the road."

I sat on the empty bed and looked up at Theo.

"Maybe you should pack my bag and look through all my stuff. You know, just to be safe."

"Right."

Theo said nothing more as he put my mind at ease and went through the scant items I owned as he packed them away.

I didn't care what either of them said, I was a dumbass.

And no one was going to convince me otherwise.

I FELT like I was living the same day of my life on repeat. Once again I'd found myself in the car, fleeing. Once again, I was mentally complaining about being in the car and swearing off road trips for the rest of my life.

"You know, I'm seriously sick of my life," I blurted.

"I bet."

"This is total bullshit."

"It is," Theo agreed.

I shifted sideways in my seat, tucked my foot under my thigh, rested my head on the back cushion, and stared at Theo driving.

"I'm lucky you look hot while you drive or all this driving around would be boring as shit."

Theo chuckled and that ended on a smile.

"I look hot while I drive?" he queried.

"Oh, yeah."

"If you say so."

"Can you tell me about what you did while you were dead?"

Again, it wasn't lost on me how absurd it was to denote a time in a person's life as "while you were dead" but there we were—two people who had returned to the land of the living. Not that I was back officially but I did feel more alive than I had since my grandmother died.

"I can't tell you the specifics," he started and I nodded even though he couldn't see me. "We moved all over Europe, Africa, and Asia. Our mission set was broad—anything from weapons, drugs, humanitarian aid, pretty much anything a terrorist could buy, trade, or sell we were after."

"Humanitarian aid?"

"Warlords love to get their hands on aid drops. One, they can sell what's in the crates and two, the people who need the aid don't get it and have to rely on the warlord for everything. Water, medicine, supplies, food. It's about controlling the population. It is amazing what a man will do for his sick child, or a son will do for his mother."

I thought back to what he said about Troy.

"You've seen otherwise decent men forced to do things they didn't want to do."

"Yeah," he whispered. "I can't judge a man for wanting to feed and protect his family. It's a vicious cycle."

It sounded like it was.

I wasn't naïve to the ways of the world. I had a clue about what went on in some third world countries, but a clue didn't mean I could fully understand the travesty. I didn't think that was something you could get from reading a book or watching a documentary. I think to fully grasp the desperation you had to see it firsthand, smell the devastation, taste the fear, hold the hand of a local, listen to them tell their story.

I had no doubt Theo lived with the greatest of understandings.

"Do you miss doing the work?"

"Yes. Do I miss the toll it took on my mental state? No. There's an expiration date to that kind of work. Both a mental and physical end date. Each day you're over there is another day closer to capture or death."

There was something in his tone that niggled.

"Were you ever captured?"

Silence.

Ugly, thick, painful silence.

I immediately regretted my question.

And I wasn't sure I was in the right frame of mind to hear the answer.

"Theo—"

"Yes. I was captured. I'm the reason Layla pulled the team out of the field and closed the program."

I was finding it hard to breathe with all the oxygen in the car turning noxious.

"I don't know what to say," I admitted.

"Nothing to say. If it wasn't for Layla going to Zane and convincing him to help her I'd be dead."

Well, thank God for Layla and Zane, too.

That mountain of misplaced guilt will be your downfall.

"Wait. Is that why you feel guilty?"

"Come again?"

"Zane said that the mountain of misplaced guilt will be your downfall. I think he was talking about your brother. But that guilt—is it because Layla closed the program?"

Holy smokes, if I thought the air was noxious before it was now infused with toxic waste.

"Yes. That and he and Kevin got captured and almost died because of me. Seems like a whole lot of risk for very little reward."

"I swear, if you weren't driving I'd punch you right in your chest, Aaron Cardon!"

"Don't call me that," he growled.

"Why not? You sure as fuck don't sound like my Theo right now. Very little reward? That reward you're talking about is your life so thank God those risks were taken. And seeing as it was Zane who called it misplaced it doesn't sound like he blames you. You didn't capture them and almost kill them. You were captured yourself. And what if they'd left you there to die? Where would that leave Layla? She was your team leader, right? What if they'd turned her down and she had to live knowing that you died because she couldn't talk Zane into helping her? Or Kira. Where would she be? You don't think she'd wonder if it was because of some bad intel she gave you that you died?"

Theo had no response, not that I thought he would.

I was pissed as hell at him and frankly I was over the whole damn day.

I stayed facing him but I closed my eyes.

I hadn't meant to fall asleep; I'd only meant to close my eyes to escape the events of that afternoon.

And since my life was still on repeat, the same thing happened as before. When we got to wherever, Theo lifted me out of the car murmuring softly, "I've got you, baby."

And just like before, I stayed asleep, still trusting I was safe in his arms.

17

I OPENED MY EYES AND FELT BRIDGET'S WEIGHT ON MY chest. The room was windowless and dark, the only light was coming from a nightlight someone had plugged into an outlet by the door. That someone had to be Layla, or Zane's wife Ivy, or maybe Garrett's wife Mellie. None of the guys would think to do it and I knew damn well none of the holding rooms at the office had nightlights in them. Zane wasn't all that concerned with prisoner care on the rare occasion we needed to detain someone overnight. Mostly the rooms were used when the guys were working and needed a place to crash for a few hours.

This was the third time I'd woken up.

The third time I stared into the dark, feeling like a monumental dick.

You sure as fuck don't sound like my Theo right now.

Aaron Cardon.

I didn't feel like Aaron anymore.

Aaron was young and naïve. He viewed the world in black and white. Right and wrong. There hadn't been shades of gray or varying degrees of wrong. He was self-righteous and narrow. He'd been out to save the world and arrogant enough to think he could.

I was no longer that man.

I knew better.

I'd seen firsthand why good men do bad things. Why men fight wars. Why women lie and scheme. I understood why mothers were compared to lionesses. I'd seen the lengths a woman would go to, to save her child.

There was no black and white out in the world.

There were no shades of gray.

There was pain and suffering and the result of that was red.

Man or woman.

Europe, Africa, or Asia.

The blood that leaked all looked the same.

Aaron Cardon was well and truly dead.

In his place Theo Jackson was born.

Bridget slid her hand from my stomach up to the left side of my chest and burrowed closer.

"You okay?" she sleepily asked.

No, I was not okay.

"I fucked up last night."

"How'd you fuck up?" she mumbled.

"I was an asshole and—"

Bridget's swift movement cut off the rest of my apology. I quickly moved my arm to give her room to slide her knee over my stomach and plant it on the mattress. And finally her hands smacking on my chest forced a grunt from my lungs.

"Listen to me," she snapped. "You don't like hearing me

call myself a dumbass; well, I don't like hearing you call yourself an asshole. Which, you can read from that, I really don't like hearing you say that you're not worth the risk. Is that why you keep waking up, because you think I'm mad about last night?"

I felt at this juncture there was no point in lying to her since she already knew I'd been restless.

"Yeah, baby. I don't like how I talked to you in the car."

Bridget tilted her head to the side and asked, "How'd you talk to me?"

"I snapped at you when you called me Aaron."

"So?"

So?

I'd been a dick after she'd had a hellacious day, which included her taking a life, and instead of taking care of her I'd made it worse.

"That shit wasn't cool."

"If you make a habit of it, I agree. You getting snippy with me when we're talking about something that bothers you is understandable. It was a shit day. I shouldn't have started that conversation but I was never mad that you were short with me. I was mad because it hurt to hear you think so little of yourself that you think Layla should've just let you die."

"It's not that," I said.

"Then what is it?"

"Maybe we shouldn't talk about this now."

"Why?" she demanded. "Because you think I'm so weak I can't take you being snippy, or because it's the middle of the night and we need to find a better time?

Because if it's the first I promise I can hack it; if it's the last then we'll wait until morning."

I didn't know what to say to that because actually 'shouldn't talk about it now' actually meant not talk about it all, ever. But she wasn't going to let me off the hook.

Fuck it.

"I'm grateful Layla was able to get Zane and Kevin to help find me. I'm grateful I'm alive. I'm grateful they're alive. My guilt runs deeper than that. Easton, Cash, Jonas, and Smith gave up the same ten years I did. And one wrong move on my part washed those years down the toilet."

"Okay, so I'm confused. In those ten years you never stopped drug deals, or weapons deals, or helped rid the world of scumbags in any way?"

"No, we did."

"So how was it a waste?"

Logically, I knew it wasn't. We'd done good work. We'd saved lives. And we'd all come home alive even if I was banged up and hanging on by a thread by the time the guys got there to rescue me.

"We weren't done," I lamely said.

"Weren't done saving the world?"

My body stilled under Bridget.

Fuck, that was like a knife to my chest.

"Theo?" she gently called and slid her hands over my chest and shoulders to curl her hands around my neck. "I want to help you but I don't know how. I don't understand where all this guilt is coming from. I've spent days with you and Easton; I know for a fact he doesn't hold a grudge."

"I was a horrible CIA operative," I admitted. "I had no business working for the agency."

"Okay."

"I joined because I wanted to make a difference. I want to *save the world*. I had no real understanding that to do my job effectively I had to live in a world where people were sacrificed like they were nothing. I had to make deals with people that were morally bankrupt—murderers, thieves, rapists—to get information on worse men, and those deals included payment and immunity. One of those payments I made was to the man who killed Kira's brother. It was years before, but I'd had dealings with him. I knowingly made a deal with a man who had killed villages of people because I needed information on a terror group who were making a dirty bomb with plans to unleash it in Mumbai. That bomb could've potentially killed hundreds, untold injuries, decimated buildings. But there I was moving my chess pieces around the board, hating every minute of it. I did my job, I played my part, but I was no longer committed to the cause because I no longer believed in it. There was no saving the world. I was simply the arrogant jackass who thought that I could do better than those who were already working the job. Turns out we need those men to make those plays, but I wasn't the man for the job."

When I was done rambling, I tipped my head back and focused on the ceiling.

"I get it."

She did?

How the hell did she get something I couldn't understand? My guilt came in waves. There were months when I could think logically about the last ten years, then there were months when I walked around sick to my stomach.

"When you were making those deals with those men

did you ever think to yourself if you just put a bullet in the man in front of you you'd rid the world of a, fill in the blank...murderer, terrorist, rapist?" Bridget questioned.

"Every. Single. Time."

"Kira's brother didn't die because of you," she whispered.

Without thinking my hands went to Bridget's hips.

I needed her off of me.

I couldn't breathe. I closed my eyes.

The room spun.

Guilt flooded in and my mind filled with visions of Finn Winters. A good brother, a good man whose beheading had been broadcasted for the world to see.

I could've stopped that. It would've meant Kira's brother would still be here.

But he was dead because I'd followed orders.

"Theo?"

I had to get the fuck out of that room.

"Come back to me, honey."

"Get off."

"I will, as soon as you open your eyes."

My eyes snapped open, Finn's face disappeared, and the room came back into focus.

Bridget scrambled off of me but didn't go far.

"That's the last fucking time we talk about that."

She came up on her knees, looked down at me, and pointed.

"You're crazy if you think that's gonna happen."

What the fuck?

"You did not kill Kira's brother. You didn't cause his death. You saved lives."

I did an ab roll, bringing me face-to-face with Bridget. "I got people killed."

She had nothing to say to that so I continued.

"I fucked with people's lives. I treated them like they were nothing."

Still nothing from Bridget. She just stared.

"I could've saved Finn."

"Like you could save the world?"

I jerked back and narrowed my eyes.

"What the fuck?" I whispered.

"You said you were arrogant by thinking you could forecast the future and somehow know that a man you were making a deal with was years later going to kill Kira's brother. That isn't arrogance. That's called having a God complex."

What the fuck?

Unfortunately she went on, "Did this man tell you his plans? Did he tell you he was going to—"

"Cut Finn's head off," I supplied.

Bridget jerked back and wrapped her arms around her middle.

"Theo," she murmured.

Fuck.

"Does Kira know?"

"That her brother's—"

"No," she cut me off. "That you feel responsible for Finn's death."

I clenched my jaw until it ached.

"She has no idea," she wrongly guessed.

"Fuck yeah, she knows."

"Obviously, she doesn't blame you."

"So? That means nothing."

Kira not blaming me didn't mean shit. I still played a part in her brother's death.

"Okay."

"Okay, what?"

"Okay, I'm not going to change your mind—"

"So you're giving up on me?" I scoffed.

Bridget scooted back, eased herself to her side, and adjusted the pillow under her head.

"Lie down, honey."

When I didn't move, she patted the bed next to her and repeated, "Lie down."

I rolled back down.

A second later she hooked her pinkie with mine.

"I'm never giving up on you," she vowed. "I'm just smart enough to know when to retreat. I'm also smart enough to know I'm not going to solve years' worth of pent-up guilt in a night or a week or a month. That's going to take time to unravel. Bottom line is, we'll untangle the rest inch by inch for however long that takes."

Bridget fell silent.

I didn't fill the silence.

Instead, I lay in the dark with her pinkie hooked around mine and wondered if Aaron was as dead as I thought he was or if I was still the same arrogant, self-righteous prick I'd been.

"I'm sorry, baby."

Bridget squeezed our pinkies together.

"I shouldn't've—"

"Shh, Theo."

God, I was such a dick.

"No, Bridget, I was harsh and that was uncalled for."

"I'm stronger than that."

She was not wrong but that didn't mean I got to treat her to my bullshit.

"I just need some time."

"Like I said, in a day, or a week, or a year. When you want to talk about it, I'll listen."

Goddamn, I loved this woman.

"You look like shit," Garrett said and tossed a stack of folders on my desk.

"What are these?" I asked, ignoring his comment.

"You first."

Jesus fuck, I didn't want to do this.

"One—"

"You know," he cut me off. "You're just like Easton. When he doesn't want to talk about something he slips into work mode and uses call signs. In here." He stopped to motion around my office. "I'm not One. I'm not the team leader, I'm not the operator, I'm me. So, brother to brother—why do you look like shit?"

I could've lied and told him I was worried about Bridget and how long we'd have to stay in one of the holding rooms. He'd believe that and wouldn't question me being stressed.

But I couldn't lie to Garrett.

"Does it get easier? The memories, I mean. Does the replay ever stop? All the shit you wish you would've done differently."

Garrett pulled out the chair in front of my desk and sat.

"Are we talking about Finn or the shit we did for the CIA or both?"

Christ, I couldn't believe we were doing this.

"Maybe we should do this later."

"Tried that. The problem is, later never comes. There's always an excuse why now's not the right time to think about it or talk about it or deal with it. I lost more years to this shit than I care to think about. The truth is the memories are always there. The replay stops when I stop pushing rewind. And that's a hard habit to break and that's exactly what it is. I'd start to heal then I'd rewind and keep it fresh. I'd have a good day, rewind. When I wanted to punish myself, rewind. Another hard truth—Yaser Said killed Finn Winters. Not me, not you, not Zane. Yaser killed him."

My lip curled into a sneer hearing that motherfucker's name.

"As far as the CIA goes, it's the CIA. Lies, manipulation, more lies, and secrets. The layers of bullshit are so deep I've learned not to expend the energy it would take to get to the truth. Did my team do good work? Fuck yeah, we did. Do I regret the years I spent working with them? Hell no. Do I regret leaving them the way I did? Yeah. But that's no longer crushing guilt, that's a regret. I've made peace with it."

Garrett had been the team leader of a CIA Ground Branch unit—Drifter Team. After the mission to rescue Finn Winters went south, Garrett bailed and left the team. Cash, Jonas, Easton, and Smith were not pissed at his deflection; they were concerned. And at no time during the ten years when I worked with them had that concern waned. Neither had their respect. So much so that when they came on to work for Patheon and I became their team leader they'd refused to allow me to be assigned the call sign One.

I'd become Two.

Garrett was, and always would be, One.

I got it then, after meeting Garrett. I understood why they respected him the way they did.

"I don't know how to make peace with the role I played in Yaser having the opportunity to kill Finn."

"I don't know how to cushion this for you," Garrett started and leaned forward, bracing his elbows on his knees. "*You* didn't play any role in how that played out. We all had our jobs to do. We did them. And that's it."

"I provided that fucker with the money he needed to start his network."

"And if it hadn't been you, Mr. Green or Mr. Black or Mrs. Blue would've. That's the mind fuck, Theo. You think you played a role when really you and I were inconsequential. Totally meaningless in a game that started long before we got there and will continue until the end of time."

My body froze while my mind raced.

Christ.

"It's time to let it go," he finished.

That may be so but I don't know how.

But I know who does.

Bridget.

Inch by inch, she'd help me untangle the mess in my head.

"Appreciate the talk."

Garrett gave me a lift of his chin and pointed to the

files.

"The answers you need are in there."

I opened the top file to an eight by ten glossy image of a badly beaten Phil Lancaster who was very obviously dead.

"Where'd they find him?" I asked instead of reading the report I knew would outline the details.

"Landfill in Wisconsin."

Well, that explained why he hadn't used his credit cards or phone.

I tossed the file to the side and opened the next.

"Who's Jaime Goodman?"

I scanned the document while Garrett answered, "Jaime is Kathy's daughter. Jaime is married to Albert Goodman who works for the Department of Justice."

"Fuck," I muttered and continued to scan Garrett's report.

"Yep. And Albert's brother Bryan works in the attorney general's office."

There it was—how Kathy was able to find Bridget and send someone after her.

The US Marshal Service falls under the Department of Justice and receives their direction from the attorney general's office. Either Albert or Bryan could've gotten Bridget's file.

"Any idea which one gave Kathy the information?"

"Could be either of them. Zane called Johnson and told him he had information on the case and requested a meeting. They'll be here tomorrow."

"Easton called in," I told Garrett.

"Cash called in, too. He said he's ordering extra room service tonight since there's been no action."

I pushed the file on Kathy Cobb to the side and started to open the third file.

"What's this one?"

"Charlie Michaels," he said. "I went over the investors. I think the Marshal Service overestimated the reach these men have. Everyone except Charlie. Zane called Charlie this morning and had a talk with him and explained that if Bridget Keller were to come back to life she would fall under Z Corps' protection."

Christ, I owed Zane.

"How'd Charlie take the news?"

"He wants a favor in return."

I felt my muscles string tight.

"You and Easton are going to Connecticut next week."

"Zane made a deal with the fucking mob," I fumed.

"Charlie has no ties to the mob. He's a very wealthy businessman with shady dealings. Zane's willing to hear him out mainly because he wants you and Easton to get a read on him. His dossier is complete." Garrett nodded at the folder. "Happy reading."

With that, Garrett stood but he made no move to leave.

"One last thing. About last night—"

"Zane already explained the power was turned off to a ten-mile grid."

"Still no excuse, brother. I didn't see the fifth man because he was in that goddamn ghillie suit and that's not an excuse, either. I fucked up."

I got it before. I fully understood why my team respected Garrett. But the more I got to know him, the deeper my respect grew. It took balls to admit you fucked up and apologize.

"Still not your fault, Garrett. He was in a yowie, there's a reason snipers use them. The access to the grid is a concern."

"As a precaution, most of the safe houses have gennies but not all. That will be addressed later this week. Ivy's ordered backup generators for the houses that don't have them."

"Good."

"Good? That's it? Have at me, brother. I fucked up and your girl had to unload a mag into some piece of shit who tried to kill her. And before you ask about the five tangos, I don't have IDs back on them yet."

Yeah, Garrett had my respect.

"And right now she's sleeping in the bed I left her in, so it's all good."

"*Is* she good?"

"She wasn't after it happened. I reminded her it was her or him and that pacified her last night but it's a Band-Aid. I'm going to watch her and if she needs it, I'll find her someone to talk to."

"Layla or Ivy. Either one of them will help get her where she needs to be."

I was more thinking along the lines of professional help but he was right—Layla or Ivy would be a good starting point.

"Mellie wants to meet her."

"She wants to meet everyone. As soon as it's safe for us to go home we'll arrange something."

"So she's staying."

That wasn't a question, but still I answered.

"Yup. I'm gonna marry that woman."

Garrett's mouth twitched before he asked, "Does she know that?"

"Not yet. I figure I'd give her a couple weeks to settle into the house first."

"Couple of weeks?" Garrett chuckled.

"Not big on wasting time, and waiting more than a couple weeks to get my ring on her finger would be a fucking waste."

"No, I meant I'm shocked you'd give her a couple of weeks. Hell, I was floored when you didn't snatch her up in the middle of the night and disappear with her before they could take her to WITSEC. I actually warned Zane he might need to start looking for your replacement in case you vanished."

A regret; that was what that was.

I never should've let her leave.

I didn't tell that to Garrett.

"Damn, Garrett, I thought you knew, there's no replacing me."

"I'm sorry, have we met? I'm *One*." He paused to point to himself. "And you're *Two*." He finished, pointing at me.

Smartass.

On a day after a shit night I didn't think it was possible yet it was...

I busted out laughing.

And because I could, I flipped Garrett off.

With that, he left.

I didn't pick up the file and get to work like I should've. Instead, I pushed back from my desk.

I needed to see Bridget.

18

"You love him?" Mellie asked from across the table.

"Totally and completely," I returned.

"What about witness protection?"

"Eff them, they almost got me killed. I'm safer with Theo."

Mellie beamed a big bright smile my way before she looked over at Layla.

Right.

I should back up.

Not even ten minutes after Theo had left me in bed snoozing, the phone on the nightstand had rung. I'd answered thinking that maybe Theo was checking on me. He'd been over-the-top apologetic when he'd woken up. And tentative. Both were unnecessary. I hadn't lied when I told him I could hack it. I knew what I was getting into when I'd pushed to have the conversation.

I'd done it then in the dark on purpose when he wouldn't be able to see me very well. I found it was easier to talk about heavy emotional things when you didn't have to stare at the person you were talking to. I started the conversation, we hit a rough patch, but in the end it had smoothed out.

When I'd told Theo everything was fine he looked skeptical. When I kissed him before he left, he wrapped his arms around me like he was afraid I was going to disappear. I didn't know how to reassure him that everything was fine, except to just be me.

So that was my plan.

But it wasn't Theo calling, it was Layla inviting me to breakfast in the conference room with her, Garrett's wife Mellie, and Zane's wife Ivy.

I was tired, mentally exhausted, and in no way in any shape to be meeting new people but I couldn't pass up the chance to meet Layla. Mellie and Ivy were simply bonuses. She told me she'd come by the room in thirty minutes. This was after she'd taken my breakfast order and assured me there was already coffee made and waiting for us.

I rushed through a shower, did the only thing I could with my hair, which was to pull it up into a ponytail, put on semi-clean but wrinkled clothes since that was all I had, and was ready by the time Layla knocked on the door.

And that was the only snag.

She'd stopped at three.

I needed five.

My heart hammered in my chest. My palms started to sweat and I was transported back to the man in one of those ghillie suits barging into the closet. I hadn't thought, I just pulled the trigger, over and over and over until the slide slammed open. Each bullet had made his body jerk—not like in the movies; it was just a slight twitch—but I watched each one hit.

I didn't see the blood until Theo came into the room. I actually didn't remember much of the time between the man hitting the floor and Theo picking me up. And the ride to the hotel was a blur.

Two more knocks had come along with Layla calling my name. When I opened the door she took one look at me, saw I was freaked, and told me she was getting Theo. It took me a few minutes to convince her I was okay.

"It's because I knocked," she said. "I read the brief this morning. I'm sorry, Bridget."

That was sweet but it wasn't her fault.

I'd explained that, too.

After that we went up to the conference room and she introduced me to Mellie and Ivy.

I was not surprised to find that Ivy was gorgeous.

And Mellie looked like the quintessential girl next door, fresh-faced and beautiful.

Then there was Layla rounding out the beauty department in her nude pencil skirt, complicated lavender blouse, and sky-high heels that made her legs look like they should be in advertisements for pantyhose.

I felt dowdy and unkept.

Yet, none of the women commented on my red, puffy, swollen eyes or my wrinkled clothes. And within minutes I was completely at ease with all of them. Hence me telling the story about my attack, finding Theo, and ending with being in love with him.

Now was now and Layla had a small grin on her face and she was studying me closely.

The longer this went on, the more nervous I got.

Theo had known Layla a long time. He spoke of her and Kira like they were special to him.

I wanted her to like me.

"Do you think it's too soon?" I asked her.

"Too soon to love Theo?" she asked in return.

I nodded.

"Why would you ask that?"

Oh, shit.

"Well... because...you're close to him."

It was her turn to nod and that made me more nervous. I should've waited to meet her until I had my wits about me. But no, I rushed the meet because I was so excited she'd called and now I was making a mess of things.

First impressions were important.

I couldn't screw this up.

"Because I know how much he cares about you," I blurted, then rushed out the rest, "and your opinion is important to him and I want you to like me."

Layla did a slow blink before she smiled.

"What I think is you have excellent instincts." She began with a nice compliment but it did nothing to assuage my worry. "Theo can and will keep you safe. But more than that, you did a good job getting yourself safe."

"You're freaking me out," I admitted.

"You know what I like about you?" she asked.

Thank God, there was something she liked.

"If I tell you I'm thrilled beyond belief that you like something about me, will you think I'm weird?"

"No, see, that right there is what I like about you. Honesty. No overthinking. No agenda. Just *honesty*. I love that after everything Theo's been through, this...you...is what he gets. So no, Bridget, I don't think it's too soon for you to love him. I think you're exactly what he needs and if you let him he'll be what you need."

"Why wouldn't I let him?"

"I just mean with men like Theo sometimes they can be a lot."

"That's an understatement," Ivy snickered.

"Tell me about it," Mellie joined.

"A lot?"

"What she's trying to say in a roundabout PC way is he's bossy just like the rest of them," Ivy said.

"Bossy's not always bad," Mellie put in. "Sometimes it can be very good."

She was correct; bossy could be very good.

"There are times I don't mind Theo being bossy," I told the women.

Mellie giggled. Ivy winked. But Layla groaned.

"Please don't go there."

"As fun as it would be to torture you I'm saving it up for Easton. His new nickname for Theo is Long John Silver," I said, then took a bite of my breakfast burrito.

It was nowhere near as good as Easton's French toast but it was still delicious.

"Long John Silver?" Layla asked. "His callsign is Two."

"Easton thinks Theo has a nine-inch penis."

"Nine inches?" Mellie laughed. "Good Lord, woman, do you need an ice pack?"

"We're not talking about this," Layla sternly said with a smile.

I took pity on Layla and said, "Okay, fine, we can change the subject."

"Oh, no, we're nowhere near done," Mellie protested. "I have questions."

"Yeah, nine inches worth of questions," Ivy snickered again.

"Come again?" Theo asked from the doorway.

Ivy burst into full-blown laughter at Theo's remark. My heart leapt into my throat and I nearly dropped my half-eaten burrito.

"You scared me half to death."

"Nine inches?"

"I was telling them about your new nickname."

I watched him do a slow blink and look at Layla.

"Don't look at me." She shrugged.

His gaze came back to me. "You okay?"

"Why wouldn't I be?"

His eyes slid through the room and then he finally made his way to me. He stopped by my chair, bent down, and kissed my temple. After that, he bent farther and took a bite out of my burrito.

"Hey!"

"Damn, that's good," he said around a mouthful of egg, cheese, sausage, and jalapeños wrapped in a nice soft tortilla. "When you're done, come by my office."

Before I could say anything Mellie mumbled, "Bossy."

Theo smiled.

"You say that like I know where your office is."

"Layla will show you."

"Will she?" Layla asked with a raised brow.

"Seeing as I was just going to our room to ask her what I

could get her for breakfast and you ruined that idea, I think you can do me the favor of bringing her by my office."

Layla didn't look the slightest bit repentant when she grinned at him and shrugged.

"See you soon, baby."

He kissed the top of my head and was gone.

The rest of our breakfast consisted of the normal getting-to-know you conversation. That was, if normal was swapping stories about kidnappings, sisters being murdered, and spy games. After listening to the three women tell me a little bit about what had gone on in their lives, suddenly my attack seemed minuscule in comparison. Not that they'd made me feel that way, but damn, Ivy Lewis was one strong woman and that went well beyond the strength she'd need to have to be married to Zane. She was just a kickass resilient woman who had lived a shit life and clawed her way out.

"Slow," Theo growled.

I didn't slow.

I went faster.

"Slow down, baby."

The sound of Theo's palm smacking my ass echoed in the room.

I slammed down on his dick and groaned.

This was me punishing Theo *and* getting my reward at the same time.

Punishing him for torturing me. I'd thought orgasm denial meant a man couldn't bring it home when he was giving you the business and you were denied the orgasm. Never in my wildest dreams did I think it would mean being edged to the brink and then denied only to be worked up and denied again. Over and over on *purpose.*

Now I knew.

And I knew because Theo had spent a goodly amount of time between my legs eating me to the verge of explosion only to pull back and use his fingers to get me close, then take those away and give me back his mouth.

By the time he told me to straddle him I was ready to lose my mind.

He felt in the mood for slow.

I needed to come so badly I was mindless in my pursuit.

His fingertips dug into my ass cheek and heat bloomed.

"You want another one?"

"Yes," I hissed.

"Fucking hell, you're magnificent," he grunted and smacked my ass hard.

Yes, bossy could be very good.

So could being bad.

I was there, so close, reaching for it with desperation, but unable to fall over the cliff into oblivion so I grunted in frustration.

"You wanna come, Bridget?"

"God, yes."

"Come with me," he commanded. "Now, baby, come with me."

His last demand was coupled with his body going solid under me, his head tipped back against the pillow, and his hand on my sore ass cheek squeezing.

My body obeyed.

Pleasure shot through me. My back arched with it. My eyes closed and tiny starbursts of light flashed behind my lids.

It was glorious.

Spectacular.

Amazingly spectacular.

When the last of my climax left me, I fell forward and face-planted on Theo's chest. His arms immediately came up and wrapped around me.

"You good?"

Oh, yeah, I was brilliant.

"No. You've ruined me. I can't even orgasm on my own. Apparently I now need you to order me to do it."

I felt him start to shake underneath me.

"I see you think that's funny. But what happens if I'm home alone and I feel the need to take care of myself?"

Theo stopped laughing and growled, "There will never be a time when you're home alone and you'll *need* to take care of yourself."

Whatever.

Moving on.

"Thank you for dinner."

"You already thanked me and again it was just Subway."

It wasn't just Subway.

"You remembered to get extra mustard and extra bell peppers."

He gave me a squeeze.

"And you remembered I like oil and vinegar."

"I remember what you like to eat."

It wasn't that.

"It's not only what I like to eat. It's that you know I only drink from a straw so you always made sure there was a box in whatever safe house I was at. It's that you remembered that certain laundry detergents make me break out into a rash so you made sure I always had Tide. You remembered all the things, but it's not really about you remembering that makes me feel good. It makes me feel loved and cared for and special."

Theo didn't say anything. Not that I expected him to. It was late, we'd both had a crazy few days. Our bellies were full. We both had sweet orgasms and it was time to sleep.

At least it was for me.

"Need you to slide off so I can get rid of this condom."

Right.

The condom.

We'd come back to the room after spending the afternoon in Theo's office to a box of condoms on the nightstand with a note taped on top. It was the worst chicken scratch I'd ever seen.

The note said: *You're welcome.*

That was it.

Theo said they were from Zane.

I thought it was strange Zane would leave condoms for his employee but I didn't question it mainly because I was grateful to have them.

I rolled to the side. Theo pressed a hard, closed-mouth kiss on my mouth before he rolled again, this time off the bed.

A few minutes later, he was back and hauled me over so my head was on his chest.

"Do you know why I remember all of those things about you?"

"Why?"

"Because you *are* special, you *are* loved, and nothing makes me happier than taking care of you."

"Do you know you're special and loved, too?"

"Yeah, baby."

"And are you going to let me take care of you while you're taking care of me?"

There was a beat of silence before...

"I'm counting on that."

"Good," I whispered and started to drift off to sleep.

19

"I've got the report on the five dead tangos." Garrett dropped a stack of papers on the table.

"All the trees," Linc muttered. "You're a computer guy and you still print shit out. Digital. Save a tree, would ya?"

Normally I'd find the banter in the conference room amusing, especially when Lincoln Parker, the man who owned three motorcycles, an Excursion, a boat, and a motorhome starts in on saving the trees—the irony is never lost on the room.

But so much today.

Johnson was due to be at Z Corps any minute and Bridget was in the building.

Having Jonas guard our room didn't make me feel any better. I didn't want Johnson anywhere near Bridget.

"They don't know she's here," Garrett told me, obviously reading my mood.

"I know but—"

"No buts. No one's going to take her. This is a friendly meeting to share intel. That's it."

He was right. That was what this meeting was supposed to be, but I couldn't shake the dread that had coated my skin since I'd woken up. Not to mention, the last time I saw Johnson it was the day he'd picked her up and taken her away. I had no desire to remember that day or to see the man ever again.

The meeting would take less than an hour. Then Johnson would be out of the building and I'd be able to breathe.

An hour.

"What'd you find?" Linc asked about the tangos.

"All five worked for Dusk. The one in the ghillie suit, Dave Sampson, spent six years in the army before he got out and went back to Utah and started working at the mine. The other four don't have service records, nothing to indicate they had any business being there, but all five are in debt out their asses and probably thought taking out a woman and her bodyguard would be easy money."

There was no such thing as easy money.

One way or another you were earning it.

"What was his MOS?" Linc asked.

"25C. Radio Operator."

"Sorry we're late, traffic was a bitch," Easton announced as he entered the conference room and plopped down in the chair next to me.

"Who's a radio operator?" Cash asked.

"The ghillie suit guy," I told him and watched his face go hard.

"When's Johnson going to be here?" Easton looked around the room waiting for an answer.

"Zane's walking him up now," Linc said, staring at his

phone. "Deputy Caraway's with him and a force multiplier named Gilbert Shaw."

The Marshals used force multipliers when needed to enhance or help on a task force, apprehension, or warrant service. Sometimes these multipliers were local law enforcement, sometimes they were contractors such as Z Corps, like when we were hired to guard Bridget.

"What the fuck?" I looked at Garrett. "Did you clear this guy?"

"Had no idea Johnson was bringing a friend."

That coating of dread thickened.

Before anything further could be said, Zane walked in the room with a face full of thunder.

Johnson didn't look all that comfortable and Caraway looked like he was miffed.

"What's going on?" I inquired.

"May we sit?" Johnson asked instead of answering me.

Zane's gaze sliced to Johnson and he shook his head.

"Not sure that's necessary at this point."

I watched as Johnson's mouth got tight and his brows pinched together.

"Goddamn, Lewis. It's not like you don't know we contract out. Hell, you've been used in the same capacity a time or two before."

I didn't know what the fuck was going on, though I could guess.

Zane didn't like surprises. None of us did, but they sent Zane into a rage when he thought someone was trying to play him. And that was what surprises were to him—sneak attacks to one-up him.

"I don't know this guy."

"Zane—"

"I don't know this guy," Zane repeated.

"I told you his name is Gil Shaw and he works for Eagle."

"This means shit to me, Johnson."

Caraway shifted uncomfortably, looking between Lincoln and Zane.

Thankfully, Garrett moved the conversation to the reason Johnson had been called in.

"What can you tell me about Albert Goodman and Bryan Goodman?"

Johnson sighed and leaned into his hand resting on the back of the chair in front of him, obviously resigning himself to standing.

"I don't know Albert Goodman, but Bryan works for the AG's office. Same last name so I'm assuming there's a relation."

"What about you, Deputy Caraway?" Garrett pushed. "Do you know Albert or Bryan?"

Caraway shook his head. "Heard the name Bryan Goodman but never met him personally."

"I don't know either of them," Gil offered without being asked.

"Why would I think you know them?" Garrett examined. "Unless Eagle has contracts with the DOJ."

Instead of answering, Gil turned to Johnson. "I thought you said they had information on Bridget Keller?"

Garrett didn't let Johnson reply.

"What about Phil Lancaster?"

"Phil Lancaster? The other pilot on Bridget's team,"

Caraway returned. "We've been looking for him, too, with no luck. Do you have his location?"

Gil's hand balled into a fist before he shoved it into his pocket. I glanced at Easton. His gaze was fixated on Gil. I looked to Cash, casually lounging back in his chair looking like he didn't have a care in the world but his eyes were sharp on Gil.

They felt it, too.

Something was off.

"Jefferson County morgue," Garrett answered.

At that news, Johnson dropped his head forward and muttered, "Fuck."

"How long has he been dead?" Caraway inquired.

"Ten days."

Gil's jaw tightened, just a fraction but that small movement said a lot.

"ME says he had fibers and hair from the body," I lied. "We should have that report in the next day or two. We'll pass it along when we get it if you want."

"I'll call the medical examiner's office." Caraway brushed off my offer.

"We used a private lab. Faster that way."

Gil could barely conceal his agitation. He no longer wanted to be here and he proved me correct when he boldly and stupidly announced, "Since you don't have any information on Bridget Keller's whereabouts we're wasting our time here."

"Who said we didn't know where Bridget Keller was?" Easton asked. "But we're not done talking about Phil yet. Did you know he was blackmailing Kathy Cobbs?"

Gil's shoulders stiffened and his left eye twitched.

"Who?"

"Johnson, pal, bud, I'm not impressed," Zane drawled. "You didn't do your homework."

"Cut this shit, Zane. Our scope of work was limited to the case. I don't have the luxury of running down every rabbit hole."

"What about you, Gil? Do you know Kathy Cobbs, Senior VP of Dusk? Albert Goodman's mother-in-law."

No sooner had Garrett finished his question than Gil's demeanor changed completely. His nerves were getting the best of him. He started to pull his hand out of his pocket, thought better of it, and shoved it back in.

"I have no idea who you're talking about," he lied.

Surprisingly, it was Caraway who put it together.

"Kathy Cobbs? Is her husband Cornelius Caine Cobbs of C3 Enterprises? Eagle does their security." Caraway paused, then asked, "What did Phil have on Kathy?"

"Drone footage he took of Kathy present at the murder of one of the Dusk employees."

Caraway nodded.

"Why do you think this ties back to Bridget?"

"Phil used Bridget's personal drone when he took the footage. Her name's on the timestamp," I explained to Caraway but kept my eyes pinned on Gil. "That, and because the man who attacked Bridget asked her what else she saw as he was attempting to choke the life out of her."

Brown hair. Brown eyes. Athletic build.

Gil Shaw had brown hair and brown eyes.

I took in the asshole now squirming under my scrutiny.

Button-up dress shirt, no tie but only the top button undone. Dark blue jeans that looked like they'd been ironed. I let my gaze continue down to his sissy ass shiny loafers that I had no doubt he paid someone to shine.

Brown suede loafers with tassels.

But it was the gum wrapper next to his shoe that caught my attention.

Spicy breath.

Fucking hell.

"Hey, One," I called. "Toss me a piece of gum, would you?"

I pushed back from the table and out of the corner of my eye I caught sight of the honeycomb rubber sole of a little boy's shoe under the table.

Goddamn, motherfucking shit.

One or both of Linc's boys were in the room.

"You know what? Never mind."

I slowly eased myself to my feet, glancing from Garrett to the table.

Understanding dawned.

Unfortunately, at the worst time imaginable, Kira Winters Cain came bouncing into the room.

"Oh, sorry, I didn't know you were in a meeting."

She turned to leave. Gil's hand shot out and grabbed her ponytail. He yanked Kira in front of him and pressed the barrel of his gun to her temple.

Eight men immediately drew their weapons.

Everyone in the room now stood facing Gil holding Kira hostage.

"This is how this is gonna go," Gil sneered. "Get me Bridget and you can have this one back."

Kira's eyes narrowed and slowly cut through the room landing on Zane. "This was not how my first day back from my honeymoon was supposed to go. And since when do we allow guns in the conference room?"

"You can take this to read the US Marshal Service is no longer on the approved carry list, Johnson," Zane quipped.

"What the fuck are you doing?" Caraway snarled. "Drop your gun and let the woman go."

"Get me Bridget!" Gil shouted and Kira winced.

"Garrett, go get her," Zane ordered.

I knew the play, yet my insides still burned at the thought. Garrett would never bring Bridget back to the room but the mere thought of this motherfucker getting his hands on her again made me insane with fury.

"Sure." Garrett made his way toward the door.

Gil moved closer to the table, taking Kira with him.

The goddamn table two little boys were hiding under.

Christ, I couldn't even look at her.

Kira.

Our Kira.

Finn's baby sister.

Cooper's wife.

Where the hell was Cooper? We were totally fucked if he came into the room. Our only hope of coming out of this without two emotionally damaged children and Kira still breathing was if her husband didn't rush into the room.

"Hey, Linc, she's still playing hide and seek with the boys, right?" Garrett asked.

Linc's neck twitched right before he turned to stone.

No one would mention his boys without reason.

"Fuck," he grunted.

"Right, I'll go get her." Garrett slipped out of the room.

"Brother," Linc started but got no more out.

Lincoln Parker was a legendary operator. Before that, he'd been a Navy SEAL. The man was known for his cold detachment but right then he was a father whose children were in harm's way and that detachment was nowhere in sight.

Not that I blamed him.

I couldn't find mine either.

"Why is no one shooting this fucker?" Kira complained.

Gil violently shook Kira, taking an already volatile situation and ratcheting it up five million degrees when she cried out in pain.

"Listen, asshole, the gun to my head is enough. You don't need to treat me like a rag doll."

"Kira, quiet, babe."

Her gaze came to me and she scowled. "I'm the one with the gun to my head. I get to say whatever the hell I want to say."

"Shut the fuck up!" Gil shouted.

Kira winced again.

I had a clear shot. I could end this now and pay for Robbie and Asher's therapy for the next twenty years when Gil's lifeless body fell and they saw their first death. Or I could miss, bullets start flying, and one of the twins got hit and Linc and Jasmin lose a son. Or Kira gets hit and Cooper's a widower after a week of marriage.

I wouldn't miss.

I'd pay for therapy.

I could end this now for all of us.

My finger slowly slid down the trigger. I felt the bend of the smooth metal under my fingertip and hoped Linc forgave me.

I never got the chance to pull the trigger.

Gil howled in pain and dropped the gun away from Kira's head.

Pandemonium ensued.

Kira drove an elbow back into Gil's gut, pushed away, and ran for the door. Johnson tackled Gil, Caraway kicked Gil's gun across the room, and Lincoln Parker dove under the table to get to his boys.

I took in the room, not understanding what the fuck just happened that made Gil drop his gun but also knowing I didn't give the first fuck.

My eyes caught on Easton. "You got this?"

"Fuck yeah," he growled.

I took off in a full sprint. Not bothering with the elevator, I hit the stairs and took them three at a time down to the basement. I ran down the hall, turned the corner, and came face-to-face with Jonas pointing his gun directly at me.

"Clear upstairs? Kira good?" he asked and lowered his gun.

"Clear," I huffed. "She's fine. Cooper's going to be pissed as fuck so I'm taking the next week off. I've got Bridget; you can go up."

Jonas nodded and moved away from the door.

Then I took the precious time needed to put Bridget at ease and knocked five times before I opened the door.

I found Bridget pacing the room.

"Is everything okay?" she asked.

"Yes."

I stalked across the room.

"You sure? You looked—"

"Like a man who gets to take his woman home?" I interjected the truth.

"It's over?"

"Yes."

"I'm free?"

"One more deal to make next week, then it's over."

"Really?"

Her smile was so huge it was blinding.

"Really."

Bridget launched herself at me. She wrapped her legs around my waist and peppered my face with kisses. That was sweet but I wanted more.

"Mouth, baby."

She pulled back, looked down, and grinned.

"Take me home, Theo."

That was the plan...

After I got my kiss.

I slid one hand off her ass, up her back, fisted her hair, and brought her mouth down to mine.

"I get to go home," she muttered against my lips.

Indeed she did.

20

Easton Spears

"Jesus, brother, did a home goods store vomit all over your house?"

I took in Theo's living room, which looked nothing like the room it was a week ago.

"Don't ask," Theo grumbled.

"Bridget?"

I couldn't imagine Bridget caring about decorating their living room. She was just happy to be there with Theo. Hell, that woman would be happy to live in a conversion van in a junkyard as long as Theo was there with her.

He was one lucky motherfucker.

Bridget was not like any woman I'd ever known.

"No, it was Kira. This is my punishment for falling in love while she was on her honeymoon."

Kira.

Yes, I could see Kira enjoying torturing Theo.

"Advice—don't fall in love if Kira's out of town," Theo went on. "It will cost you a fortune in paint, pillows, towels, these fluffy rugs that apparently go in the bathroom so your feet are warm while you brush your teeth, and dishes. Lots and lots of fucking serving platters."

"Not planning on ever falling in love so I'm safe."

"Right. See, you don't plan on doing shit, it just happens."

I knew all too well how falling in love worked.

Thankfully, Bridget came into the room with her phone to her ear, cutting off a conversation I wanted no part of.

"Great! We can't wait. I'm so excited."

Bridget ended the call and smiled.

"Hey, Easton."

"What's up, Birdie Bird?"

"Oh, nothing, just coming back from the dead. You know, the usual."

Damn, I adored this woman.

"Was that Troy?" Theo asked.

"Yeah. He'll be here next Monday and he's staying until Wednesday."

"Good news, baby. We'll have everyone over."

"I bet he'd like that."

Troy the truck driver. Who would've thought Theo would welcome a stranger into his home? The Theo before Bridget sure as shit wouldn't have. Bridget's Theo, however, caved to her every request.

"You're going to spoil her if you're not careful," I teased.

"Don't you have to go to Connecticut to ensure this Charlie guy isn't going to murder me?"

"Not fucking soon," Theo grunted.

I gave Bridget a wink of encouragement. Watching her wind up Theo was one of my favorite things.

"When's Kira coming over?"

"She and Mellie will be here in about ten minutes."

"We can wait," I suggested.

"Nope. You two go so you can get back."

Theo started across the room and I took that as my cue to leave the lovebirds to say goodbye in private.

"See ya, Gidget."

"Don't call me that," she groused. "I let Birdie slide but Gidget is a hard no unless you want me to start calling you Silverback."

"Silverback?"

"I did some research. The Silverback has the smallest penis and testicles of male apes, coming in at four centimeters. Seems fitting."

Yeah, Theo was a lucky motherfucker.

"That's me, a small-penis ape. Not all of us have big dicks to swing around."

"Is that why you're single?"

Ouch.

"No, Gidget, I'm single because I enjoy the many flavors the world has to offer. Why eat vanilla for the rest of my life when I can have chocolate tonight, peach tomorrow, and sorbet the day after?"

"Maybe because one day when you're done gorging yourself you'll be sitting in a lazy boy lonely and overweight with a mouthful of cavities wishing you hadn't binged on chocolate, peach, and sorbet."

Ouch again.

"Don't worry. I brush after every meal. But your

concern for my dental health is appreciated." I glanced over at Theo. "Meet you outside, brother."

CHARLIE MICHAELS' ten-thousand-square-foot mansion was the very definition of gluttony.

It didn't scream money. It slapped you in the face and shoved it down your throat.

"I have a problem I'm hoping you can solve," Charlie said and tapped the thumb drive on his desk. "You do this for me, I'll forget I had millions invested in Raven. Millions I lost."

Millions he'd earned from shady business dealings. Not that I'd remind him of that when Theo was vibrating with pent-up rage. Though I had to admit Theo had handled the whole situation in the conference room better than I would've if the man who'd attacked my woman was standing in front of me. I'm not sure I'd be able to live with him sitting behind bars instead of being buried, but the plus side to Gil Shaw being alive was he was a tattletale. Heads were rolling from the DOJ, Attorney General's office, Marshal Service, Dusk Mining Company, and C3.

Oh, what a tangled web we weave when mommy offs a worker so he couldn't report OSHA violations. The hilarious part was the OSHA fine wouldn't have put a dent in the company's profits. But it sure as fuck cost Kathy Cobbs a lot of money and her freedom.

"What's your problem?" I asked.

"Everything you need is on this." Charlie tapped the drive again with a manicured finger and I fought a lip curl.

As a rule of thumb I didn't trust a man with soft hands. A man who paid to have his nails trimmed and filed was suspect.

Charlie Michaels was suspect.

"Take this and my daughter—"

"Your daughter?" I interrupted him.

"Yes, my daughter Nebraska. She'll help you."

Nebraska?

Who the fuck named their child after a state?

Just then a woman walked into the room. Her beauty was striking but her jeans, flip-flops, and plain tight white t-shirt were outrageously out of place in the gaudy mansion.

I waited for her to apologize to Mr. Michaels for the interruption.

That apology never came.

"I'm packed and ready," the woman said.

"Good. Nebraska, this is Easton Spears and Theo Jackson. They're going to help."

We are?

We hadn't agreed to terms.

Nebraska turned her pool-blue eyes in my direction and gave me a tight but still sweet smile.

"Thank you so much. I really appreciate it."

Every word was laced with relief.

"No problem."

Theo's head snapped to the side and he gave me his patented 'are you fucking crazy' look.

"No problem?" he repeated as a question.

Oh, there was a problem. I just didn't have the first clue that the problem was about to turn my life inside out.

ALSO BY RILEY EDWARDS

Riley Edwards

www.RileyEdwardsRomance.com

Takeback

Dangerous Love

Dangerous Rescue

Dangerous Games

Dangerous Encounter

Dangerous Mind

Dangerous Hearts

Gemini Group

Nixon's Promise

Jameson's Salvation

Weston's Treasure

Alec's Dream

Chasin's Surrender

Holden's Resurrection

Jonny's Redemption

Red Team - Susan Stoker Universe

Nightstalker

Protecting Olivia

Redeeming Violet

Recovering Ivy

Rescuing Erin

The Gold Team - Susan Stoker Universe

Brooks

Thaddeus

Kyle

Maximus

Declan

Blue Team - Susan Stoker Universe

Owen

Gabe

Myles

Kevin

Cooper

Garrett

The 707 Freedom Series

Free

Freeing Jasper

Finally Free

Freedom

The Next Generation (707 spinoff)

Saving Meadow

Chasing Honor

Finding Mercy

Claiming Tuesday

Adoring Delaney

Keeping Quinn

Taking Liberty

Triple Canopy

Damaged

Flawed

Imperfect

Tarnished

Tainted

Conquered

Shattered

Fractured

The Collective

Unbroken

Trust

Standalones

Romancing Rayne

Falling for the Delta Co-written with Susan Stoker

AUDIO

Are you an Audio Fan?

Check out Riley's titles in Audio on Audible and iTunes

Gemini Group

Narrated by: Joe Arden and Erin Mallon

Red Team

Narrated by: Jason Clarke and Carly Robins

Gold Team

Narrated by: Lee Samuels and Maxine Mitchell

The 707 Series

Narrated by: Troy Duran and C. J. Bloom

The Next Generation

Narrated by: Troy Duran and Devon Grace

Triple Canopy

Narrated by: Mackenzie Cartwright and Connor Crais

More audio coming soon!

BE A REBEL

Riley Edwards is a USA Today and WSJ bestselling author, wife, and military mom. Riley was born and raised in Los Angeles but now resides on the east coast with her fantastic husband and children.

Riley writes heart-stopping romance with sexy alpha heroes and even stronger heroines. Riley's favorite genres to write are romantic suspense and military romance.

Don't forget to sign up for Riley's newsletter and never miss another release, sale, or exclusive bonus material.

Rebels Newsletter

Facebook Fan Group

www.rileyedwardsromance.com

facebook.com/Novelist.Riley.Edwards
instagram.com/rileyedwardsromance
bookbub.com/authors/riley-edwards
amazon.com/author/rileyedwards

Printed in Great Britain
by Amazon

52328733R10149